ARCHANGEL

Scott Harrison

First published in November 2012
by Big Finish Productions Ltd
PO Box 1127, Maidenhead, SL6 3LW
www.bigfinish.com

Blake's 7 Producer for Big Finish: David Richardson
Executive Producers for Big Finish: Nicholas Briggs and Jason Haigh-Ellery

Executive Editor for B7 Media: Andrew Mark Sewell
Managing Editor: Jason Haigh-Ellery

Production Editor: Xanna Eve Chown
With thanks to Peter Anghelides and John Binns

Cover design: Anthony Lamb

ISBN: 978-1-78178-022-0
ebook: 978-1-78178-023-7

A CIP catalogue record for this book is available from the British Library

Typeset in Baskerville

Printed and bound in Great Britain by Biddles Ltd, King's Lynn, Norfolk
www.biddles.co.uk

This book is for my wife, Linzi

BLAKE'S 7 NOVELS
FROM BIG FINISH

ARCHANGEL

CONTENTS

FIVE YEARS AGO

They moved silently beneath a starless sky, eight of them altogether; shapeless forms hidden beneath black, featureless uniforms.

Pale light flashed across the smooth, domed peaks of their combat helmets as they pushed their way through the forest clearing, following the steady curve of the river northwards. The narrow trail that wound down to the water's edge was slippery underfoot and had to be taken one at a time. The only sound as they clambered down from the rocky outcrop was the rush of wind high in the leafy canopy overhead, of muffled breathing beneath thick protective face-guards.

They emerged from the trees, stopping at the edge of the sandy bank, the dark river water knotted with ripples as it flashed past, inches from where they stood. They were making good time and could afford a brief rest. Not that there was any real hurry. The traitor and his family weren't going anywhere, not in this weather. An icy wind was blowing down off the mountains, bringing with it a tangle of swollen, grey cloud; there'd be a hard frost on the ground by morning, perhaps even an inch or two of snow.

Space Captain Garrin pushed his way slowly through the small collection of troopers, the crunching of the loose stone and shale beneath his boots like an artillery barrage in the silence of the forest. He stopped a little further up the bank and lifted his visor, peering into the gloom.

The sky was growing darker, the sun little more than a blazing scar beyond the trees to the west. In the dying light he could just make out the broken path of rocks that stretched across the river, from one bank to the other, jagged peaks piercing the surface of the turbulent water.

'There…' Garrin hissed, a grin pushing at the corners of his mouth. He half-turned, eyes scanning the dark knot of shapes a few metres behind him. He spotted the tall, slightly stooped frame of his second–in–command almost immediately, sitting on a rock to one side of the group, legs folded awkwardly in front of him. 'Darvik. Get over here.'

A second or two later, the Section Leader appeared at his side, tugging off his helmet and tucking it into the crook of his arm.

Garrin stood in silence, his eyes tracking along the gentle sweep of the river ahead, watching as it twisted down into the valley, spiralling through the trees until it disappeared into the hills beyond. Then he jabbed a finger towards the growing swell of shadows. 'That patch of scrubland there, where the river narrows… that's north west isn't it, lad?'

Darvik nodded. 'Yes, sir – give or take. According to the map, the river skirts the edge of the forest for another four or five miles in that direction, before it hits the mountain range.'

'Good. Then that's where you'll take your squad,' the Captain told him. 'If you keep the water in sight at all times, and stick to the marsh ground for a good mile or so, that should bring you out to the north of the ruins.'

Darvik thought about this for a moment, then gave his superior another terse nod. 'Might be a problem for the lander, sir. All that greenery. It could miss us out there.'

'Let Control worry about that, son. You just concentrate on getting the "package" delivered.' Garrin slammed his visor into place and jerked his head back towards the spot where the men were waiting.

The Section Leader saluted and disappeared off towards the troopers, fixing his helmet back into place as he went.

Within minutes, the men were moving again, picking their way slowly, carefully, across the river; water frothing around their boots as they waded from rock to rock. On the opposite bank, the garrison peeled off into two groups of four. The first plunged on ahead, deeper into the forest, while the second group, led by Darvik, edged along the loose shale bank towards the dark tangle of scrubland further up the river.

As the troopers pushed on, breaking the tree line and heading for the old stone ruins beyond, the first flakes of snow fell from the sky.

It was getting colder. Kodyn was sure of it. Either that or the stimulants Blake had given him were beginning to wear off.

He pulled the collar of his tunic tighter around his neck and reached for another branch to throw on the fire. The flames were getting low again. T; the wood he'd collected together was too damp to burn properly; it did very little except extinguish the flames and fill the interior of the old building with long, noxious fingers of black smoke. Kodyn cursed silently. The smoke was probably visible for miles in all directions, even this far into the forest. If a security patrol should pass by now...

If he wasn't careful his stupidity was going to get them all killed.

Kodyn leant back against the pitted stonework of the wall and watched his daughters as they slept. They looked so fragile curled up by the fire, hidden beneath their mother's rough, woollen shawl. So small and helpless. They could easily be mistaken for a pile of discarded clothes, strewn carelessly on the hard, stone floor.

How could he have done this to them? He said he would protect them, had given them his word, promised to get them out of the Dome and safely off the Earth, perhaps even as far as the outer colonies. He didn't really care where they went, as long as they were far enough away from the mood suppressants and artificial stimulants that the Federation was pumping into the bodies of his family, polluting the minds of his children, twisting their reason.

Blake had told him where to go: five klicks due north, just beyond the thick belt of trees, there would be a transporter ship waiting for them. He'd given him a homing device, its tiny sensor-core locked onto the ship's transponder signal.

'Use it sparingly,' Blake had told him, 'and only when you've passed beyond the range of the Dome's detector field. Activate it before then and you'll have a tracking party down on you so fast you won't have time to run or hide.'

The contact had been waiting for them by the service hatch in the lower levels, just as Blake had promised. Kodyn couldn't remember the man's name now – he thought it might have been Dev, or possibly Del – though it hardly seemed to matter; there'd been very little time for introductions at any rate. Whatever the man's name, he'd said very little to them, just reiterated Blake's instructions, then quickly bypassed the micro-electronic seals of the outer hatchway so that it could be opened without tripping the security circuits in the Dome's computer room.

Beside him on the ground was an old plastic satchel that contained the homing device, an electro-topographical map of the surrounding area, and a small laser pistol that Blake had given him the night before they had left the Dome. The pistol was for emergencies, Blake had told him. A last resort. Should it ever come to that. His friend's eyes had been cold, unblinking, and it had taken a moment for the words to truly sink in. When they had, Kodyn had snatched his hand away from the gun as though it were white hot. He'd taken it anyway, despite how wrong it had felt in his hands. It had been the first time he'd held a gun.

He slipped it from the front pocket of the satchel and checked the clip again, hands trembling as the effects of the stimulants began to wear off.

On the other side of the fire his wife, Lyssa, stirred fitfully in her sleep, causing Kodyn to almost drop the pistol in fright. He waited for her to settle back down again before he clicked the safety bolt into the *on* position, then stuffed the weapon into the pocket of his tunic. It felt heavy and awkward lying there inside his clothing and he tried his best to ignore it.

They'd got away from the Dome and were safe, for now. That was the most important thing. At first light the four of them would be making for the transporter ship again, and after that he wouldn't need the pistol. He could dump it in the undergrowth before boarding the vessel, or hand it over to one of the crew. Whichever way, he'd be rid of it soon. Blake had only given it to him as a precaution, he told himself. He wouldn't need to use it.

Kodyn forced himself to his feet, then walked slowly through each of the crumbling rooms in the building, hand wrapped protectively around the handle of the laser pistol nestled in his pocket. He stopped for a while when he reached the hallway, one foot resting on the bottom step of the wide staircase. The room was huge; the ceiling arching high overhead reminded Kodyn of the great Archive Halls back in the Dome. He shuddered, peering upwards into the darkness that collected on the first floor landing, and thought briefly about checking the upstairs rooms. Instead, he turned and headed for the front door.

Outside, the air shimmered in the cold. Along the edges of the forest clearing a thin, grey mist was pooling, stirred only by a sharp breeze that tumbled down off the mountains.

Kodyn stood in the deep blue darkness of twilight, face turned up towards the stars, and fought back the tears. Every time he closed his eyes he kept seeing that one frozen moment: the image of his daughters, curled in front of the fire, wrapped up in their mother's shawl for warmth.

It almost broke his heart to recall how confused and afraid they'd been when he'd woken them the night before, when he'd told them to get out of bed and get dressed. Tala, just twelve years old, had stood in the hallway comforting her sister Katri, younger than her by four years, as their mother raced around the living-unit, grabbing things off shelves, out of cupboards, and thrusting them into the backpack. Both girls had been so silent as they'd stepped through the open service hatch and out into the cold night air for the first time, Tala clinging tightly to his side not daring to let go, her eyes so wide, so full of confusion and fear.

Snow was falling now and Kodyn realised that his hands and feet were beginning to ache from the cold. He turned and walked back into the ruined building, returning to his family and the warmth of the dying fire.

There was a spare blanket-roll in the corner of the room, along with a flask of water and a container of hastily packed food. Kodyn unrolled the blanket and laid it on the ground next to Lyssa, then ate a few protein biscuits from the food container. He wasn't really that hungry; it was more to stop his stomach from cramping than anything else.

Before he settled down, he checked that his daughters were warm and comfortable, tucking the covers up high around their chins and kissing them lightly on the forehead. Then he lay down beside his wife. He was teetering on the edge of sleep when he heard movement in the other room and his eyes flew open.

Snowflakes drifted down from the tangle of dark cloud. Only a handful at first, tossed on the cold breeze, then gradually growing faster, heavier.

Darvik licked his lips nervously, waiting for the Captain to get into position and give the signal. He could feel the cold trickle of sweat down his spine despite the biting wind that tugged at his thin uniform.

'*Sir!*'

The voice was little more than a hiss, coughed out from between cold, dry lips. It came from somewhere behind him, a little further along the ridge. Darvik swung his head around, squinting into the gloom.

The trooper who had spoken gestured towards his own face, then at the ruins in front of them. It was a signal: *Target in sight.*

Darvik flattened himself against the frozen ground, eyes scanning the area ahead. The trooper was right. He could see the traitor standing out there amongst the ruins, his deep crimson tunic blazing like a beacon amidst the falling flecks of white. He didn't seem to be doing anything, just standing there, a laser pistol clutched absently in his hands. His head was turned away so Darvik couldn't see his face clearly, but he seemed to be staring out across the tops of the trees towards the mountains in the north.

Darvik waited for a minute or two, but the traitor continued to gaze out into the darkness, face titled upwards, unmoving. The Section Leader pushed himself backwards, shuffling back down the ridge until he was hidden behind the ruins again. As soon as he was out of sight, he scanned the ridge again to make sure that his men were in position.

The trooper to his left had swung his rifle from his shoulder and was slotting a new cartridge into the grip-feed, his eyes on the Section Leader. Darvik signalled quickly, circling the air with his forefinger, then pointing to the far side of the ruined building: *Circle around behind the target.* Then he held up five splayed fingers, before bringing them quickly together into a tight fist: *Wait five minutes, then move in.*

The trooper nodded, slinging the rifle across his shoulders once more, before creeping silently away along the ridge.

After a few seconds, Darvik moved forward again, sliding along on his stomach. He had to assume that Captain Garrin had seen the traitor too and was holding position just beyond the treeline. If that was the case then he was probably waiting for the target to move a little closer, away from the ruins, before risking taking a shot. Darvik turned to signal the two remaining troopers on his right, but a sudden movement caught his eye, and he froze.

The traitor had spun quickly on his heel and was walking away from them, back towards the broken entrance to the building. At the same time Garrin's group broke cover, emerging silently from out of the dense curtain of trees, and disappearing amongst the jagged line of stones.

Gripping his rifle, Darvik signalled for the other troopers to follow him, before pushing himself up onto the ridge and darting across the open ground towards the ruined building.

The first bolt hit Lyssa in the chest, jerking her off her feet and slamming her backwards into the wall; the second tore her head from her shoulders, sending spumes of dark blood spraying into the air.

Tala began to scream, her eyes wide with shock as she reached instinctively for the sleeping form of her sister.

More uniformed men came pounding into the room from the doorway opposite as Kodyn fumbled for the laser pistol in his tunic pocket. The material tore as he tugged the barrel free, swinging it clumsily upwards in the direction of the approaching troopers. He squeezed the trigger but the shot went wild as the man at the front of the group, a tall, awkward-looking youth, knocked the gun aside with the barrel of his rifle, before punching Kodyn in the face with his free hand.

There was a loud crack as his nose shattered beneath the impact, causing him to stagger backwards against the wall. The gun skittered across the floor as Kodyn slid down onto one knee, his hands clawing at the crumbling brickwork in a desperate attempt to keep himself upright; around him the room was heaving like the deck of a starship making an emergency planetfall.

The room was full of Federation troopers now, circling slowly towards the centre of the room, keeping themselves between him and the doorways at either end of the room.

He could hear Katri. She was awake now and sobbing uncontrollably. The noise brought the world back into sharp focus, giving him the strength to fight against the tide of unconsciousness that threatened to break over him. Kodyn shook his head and glanced towards the sound, to where Katri sat clinging to her sister in terror.

Just behind them he could see the body of their mother, slumped against the wall like one of Tala's discarded dolls, one hand outstretched towards her daughters, as though she were trying to reach them. The blood that stained the wall above her was so vivid in the flickering light from the fire, so *red*. It was as though it were the only colour left in the world, everything else was constructed in drab blacks and grubby whites. Tears stung the corners of Kodyn's eyes. He felt like screaming until his throat was ragged and raw, until all the breath had been ejected from his lungs, all the life expelled from his body.

That's when he saw his gun. It was lying a few metres away, exactly where he had dropped it, half-hidden behind a pile of fallen masonry.

Kodyn kicked away from the wall and fell forward, one hand reaching towards the gun, the other clawing at the empty air, desperately trying to hold on to something, anything, that would halt his fall.

The tall trooper struck out at him again, this time fetching him a good whack on the base of his skull with the butt of his laser rifle, and Kodyn went down.

The last thing that Kodyn heard were his young daughters' screams as the Federation troopers dragged them out of the ruined building and into the bitter night air. Then something hit him a second time and Kodyn tumbled down into darkness.

PART ONE
Ghosts

CHAPTER ONE

The flight deck seemed different without Gan: emptier, somehow incomplete.

Vila Restal had spent a great deal of his time since Gan's death trying to make up his mind whether it was worth sticking around on the *Liberator* anymore. Sure, he liked Blake, there was no doubt about that, even trusted him still – well, up to a point – but he couldn't help feeling that things had suddenly and irrevocably changed.

For a start he didn't feel safe anymore, not without Gan watching his back. Whatever the situation, he was a good man to have on your side, even with the limiter implant in his head. Vila had always said that a man like Olag Gan was worth his weight in Ephesian fire-gems.

Or, at least, he had been. Before he'd got himself killed at the Central Control back on Earth.

Correction: before *Blake* had got him killed.

By rights none of them should have stuck with Blake after that. Once they were aboard the *Liberator* again, and heading for the outer systems with the Earth at their backs, they should have divided up the fortune – the one Jenna had discovered, on the lower decks, behind the security door at the farthest end of the bulkhead – and gone their separate ways. No-one would have blamed them; in fact it would have probably been for the best.

Vila craned his neck, peering back over his shoulder at the empty navigation control module where Gan always sat.

They were supposed to be indestructible, weren't they? A lone voice shouting in the darkness, unable to be silenced… or something along those lines. That was the story being told in the outer colonies, at any rate. Trouble was, the crew of the *Liberator* had been hearing it for so long now they'd started to believe it themselves. Especially Blake. And now they'd paid a terrible price for their arrogance.

An oval panel on the far wall flickered suddenly to life: a myriad of pale lights chasing one another across its smooth, convex surface. The voice that accompanied it was cold and expressionless, almost a parody of the human voices that currently inhabited the spaceship.

'INFORMATION,' Zen announced to the almost empty flight deck. '*LIBERATOR* IS NOW IN FIXED ORBIT 1,000 SPACIALS ABOVE SURFACE OF PLANET GERISS II, AND OUT OF RANGE OF FEDERATION OUTPOST SCANNING SYSTEMS.'

Vila looked up slowly, as though registering the presence of the ship's computer for the first time. 'So what?' he shrugged, flicking idly at the control panel in front of him. 'They'll find us eventually and kill us one by one, just like poor old Gan. Sitting out here won't make much difference. You mark my words, Zen, this is the beginning of the end for us all.'

'PLEASE RE-STATE PARAMETERS OF YOUR LAST INSTRUCTIONS.'

'Oh, never mind,' Vila snapped back. 'Hold current position and bring the long range detectors online.'

'CONFIRMED.'

On the forward viewscreen, the planet spun in the inky darkness like a vast, sparkling emerald, the occasional patch of wispy grey-white cloud fluttering across its surface. Vila eyed the scene disdainfully for a second or two, before adding, 'And turn the screen off.'

'CONFIRMED.'

The viewscreen blinked off obediently, leaving Vila with nothing but his brooding thoughts and sullen temper for company. For a while he let the steady thrum of the *Liberator*'s engines wash over him, clearing his head.

Perhaps it wouldn't be such a bad idea after all, cutting his losses and jumping ship at the first available planet. *Well, maybe not the* first *available planet,* Vila mentally amended. *It would have to have certain amenities if I was going to be spending the rest of my life there. Certain inbuilt luxuries, designed to make life just that little bit more tolerable. Like a gambling suite. And a bar. Oh, and girls, of course. Lots of girls. After all, 'the rest of my life' is such a long time, I'll need the odd distraction or two.*

Come to think of it, Vila had heard of this one place, outside the Federation, called Freedom City…

'I hope I'm not disturbing you. You're obviously very busy at the moment.'

The voice broke Vila's concentration, shattering all his fantasies into tiny little pieces – just as it was getting interesting, too. With a sigh he opened his eyes and looked around. Jenna was standing at the entrance to the flight deck, hands on hips, her head cocked inquisitively to one side.

'You *are* disturbing me, actually,' Vila told her, annoyance flecking his voice. 'I've got some important decisions to make and I need to think about them carefully.'

Jenna's eyes narrowed. 'Funny how you always snore when you're thinking about important things.'

'Since when did it become a crime for a man to have dreams? Aspirations?' Vila asked quickly. 'Is it too much to ask to want something better than this?' And he flapped a hand at the flight deck around him.

Jenna slid into the pilot module and checked something on her instrument panel. 'You won't have *anything* if a flotilla of Federation attack ships sneak up on us.' She looked up, a smile fluttering across her lips. 'None of us will. We'd be too busy orbiting this planet in tiny little bits to care.'

'Everything's fine. Zen's taking care of all that.'

'But it still needs one of us to monitor the situation,' Jenna said. 'All it takes is for one momentary lapse of concentration, Vila, and we'll all end up like…' She trailed off.

Vila's voice was barely audible above the background chatter of the computer systems. 'Say it. Just like Gan.' There was a genuine sadness in his voice; he really did miss his old friend. 'You can't tell me that this hasn't changed things. Gan died because of Blake. Doesn't that worry you, even a little?'

'What worries me more is that you didn't see this coming.' Avon had appeared at the top of the steps that led down onto the flight deck, a large, semi-translucent rectangular box clutched in his hands.

He took the steps carefully, clutching the box tightly to his body, stopping as he drew level with the pilot module. He turned to look at Jenna. 'That *none* of you saw this coming.' He walked past her, placing the box on the console in front of Zen, then he half-turned, glancing sideways at Vila. 'Just count yourself lucky that it was Gan that died back there on Earth and not you.' Avon paused, then added with a smile, 'although your turn may come sooner than you think. You're all in this until the bitter end. Blake will see to that.'

'And you're just tagging along for the ride, I suppose?' Jenna asked. 'Tell me, Avon, if you hate Blake that much why are you still here?'

Avon pulled a small operating key from his tunic pocket and held it in the air between thumb and forefinger. 'Staying with Blake has certain... advantages. For the moment, anyway.'

He slotted the key into a small recess on the top of the box and it immediate burst into life. Tiny lights fluttered within its depths as rows of vacuum-sealed memory processors began to hum with power. As the box began to glow with a pale, internal light, there was an odd, strangulated cough, as though the thing was trying to clear its electronic throat.

When Avon addressed the box, he did so without looking at it, as though he didn't much care for it. 'Orac, transfer all military communications beamed out of Centero in the last twenty-four hours to the main viewscreen, then decode.' He paused, considering for a moment or two. 'Prioritise all messages tagged Security Code Alpha One. Filter out anything that doesn't contain the word Archangel.'

'Might I remind you that my programme functions and capabilities extend infinitely further than as a mere communications device. Asking me to perform such tasks is not only an insult but also a complete waste of my time and talents.' The supercomputer spoke in the clipped, almost waspishly curt manner of its creator, Professor Ensor, a brilliant man, but insufferably arrogant – a characteristic he'd instilled in his creation before he died.

'Personally I don't care if you remind me of it or not,' Avon told it, 'as long as you transfer the messages to the screen while you're doing it.'

'Oh, very well,' Orac replied irritably.

As the main viewscreen sprang into life Avon ordered Zen to bring the ship down to an orbital path of 800 spacials, hoping to use the planet's ionosphere as a camouflage against long-range Federation detectors.

'You'd better tell our illustrious leader to come to the flight deck,' Avon said, once the *Liberator*'s retros had begun to manoeuvre them into a tighter orbit. 'Thanks to Blake's old friend Fleet Officer

Tobin, I think I may have just found his next opportunity to get you all killed.'

'It would help if I knew what I was looking at.'

Data flickered across the viewscreen in three neat columns; most of the information concerned itself with ship transponder frequencies, fleet positions and troop reassignment. All of it was good solid stuff, worth passing across to the separatist groups on the outer worlds, but so far Blake failed to see why Avon was making such a fuss about it.

'And nothing strikes you as odd?' Avon asked, pointing at the undulating data threads. 'Look again, Blake. Training manoeuvres, military flight plans, cargo security details, all standard operational procedures and routine Federation intelligence. Yet everything up there on that screen was Alpha One security-coded using an encrypted cypher. Virtually impossible to break, unless you have one of these.' He pointed across at Orac whose lights began to flash with barely contained annoyance.

There was a moment's silence, then Blake's forehead crumpled into an impatient frown. 'Well, don't keep us in suspense,' he said. 'I know you're dying to tell us all.'

Jenna and Cally exchanged a smile.

'Orac was able to filter out several strands of encoded data embedded within each of these messages,' Avon said. 'Strands purposefully hidden inside the data streams, and all containing the same word, used over and over again: Archangel. It would seem your friend, Tobin, was right.'

Blake stopped pacing. '*Archangel?*' There was something about that name that rang alarm bells somewhere at the back of his mind. It had been gnawing away at him ever since they'd received Tobin's message twelve hours earlier. But where had he heard it before?

'Does it mean something to you?' Avon asked.

'I'm not sure…' Blake responded. 'Maybe. Although there's something I'm not quite seeing. Orac, what exactly is Archangel? Could it be some kind of weapon?'

'It is possible,' said Orac. 'Although I have found no evidence so far to support this.'

'So what have you found?' Avon asked.

'Archangel is the code name of a Federation project known only to those with the very highest level of security clearance.' Orac said.

'What sort of project?' asked Blake.

'I am continuing to search but a number of security firewalls are proving particularly problematic, even for me,' said the computer. 'All I can be certain of is that it was set up five years ago then shut down somewhat abruptly two years later. The order came directly from the President of the High Council himself.'

'Things must have gone seriously wrong for the President himself to step in.' Blake said. 'Why was it stopped?'

'I am unable to find a reason,' said Orac. 'There are gaps in the information that appear to have been made deliberately.'

'Which would seem to imply that no one was supposed to know why it was stopped,' said Blake.

'Or that the project existed in the first place,' said Avon. 'That's what makes it so intriguing – that of course, and the fact that these messages are recent. Which suggests that someone, somewhere is trying to start up the project again.'

'*Someone*?' said Cally. 'I take it you mean outside the Federation?'

'Or someone acting without the High Council's authority,' said Avon. 'This "someone" is trying to start up the project again without drawing attention to themselves.'

'That doesn't sound good,' said Cally. 'Do we have any idea who was sending these messages?'

'Or receiving them?' Jenna added.

'No,' said Avon. 'To both questions. I had Orac run a trace for any info-tags or serial idents on the strands, but there's a hole in the data where they've been removed.'

'Whoever it is, they're certainly not taking any chances.' Blake said. He folded his arms across his chest and stepped closer to the screen, peering intently at the flickering streams of data.

'Or is that what *he* wants us to think?' The voice belonged to Vila.

It was the first time he'd spoken since Blake had arrived on the flight deck. He was sitting in the curved seating area in front of the flight modules dealing himself a dummy hand from a deck of Auron cards. Blake had assumed that he hadn't been listening to their conversation.

'*He*? You think this might be down to Travis?' Blake asked.

Vila flipped over a yellow double six and threw it onto the table with a sigh. His hand was now at forty-four with mixed colours; he'd busted himself out of the game. He looked across at the viewscreen as he scooped the cards up off the table and returned them to the deck.

'It's exactly the kind of thing he would try, if you ask me,' Vila said. 'I know none of you *are* asking me.' He glanced at Avon. 'And most of you don't even care what I have to say...'

Impatiently Jenna held up a hand, cutting him off. 'Get to the point, Vila.'

'The point is, Travis knows we're listening. He even knows that Orac is capable of intercepting all communications in and out of Centero. Unpicking a few encrypted threads is child's play to him.' Vila stuffed the deck of cards into his pocket and shuffled over to the small group clustered around the main viewscreen. 'He's been on our backs for a while. Now Gan's dead, he'll be eager to finish the job.'

'One down, five to go,' Jenna remarked carelessly, regretting it the moment she saw the flash of pain and guilt in Blake's eyes.

'We're no longer indestructible, Blake,' Vila said. 'The Federation know that now. And more importantly Travis knows it.'

As much as it pained him to admit it, Blake knew that Vila was probably right. Something like this was certainly Travis's style: feed them false information too tempting to ignore, lure them to a set of predetermined co-ordinates, then ambush them with a fleet of Hunter Killers. Unoriginal, yes, bordering on the unimaginative, but then Space Commanders weren't exactly known for their imagination, only their ruthlessness and unswerving arrogance. It had to be Travis. This thing had his fingerprints all over it.

But Blake also knew that he really had no choice in the matter. They *had* to take the risk. What if his first instincts were correct and Archangel was some sort of new weapon? It wasn't like the Federation hadn't tried it before. In fact it hadn't been long since they'd stumbled across a project known as Imipak – a weapon so lethal it could kill at exceptional distances. If Servalan still had possession of that they'd probably all be dead by now. He really wouldn't put it past Space Command to restart the project again, especially now that the dust had settled.

Or perhaps it was some new type of brain-conditioning device? That would also make sense, particularly after all those disturbing stories Blake had heard recently, coming out of the new colonies.

No, they had to find out what Archangel meant and why the Federation was going to such extraordinary lengths to keep it hidden. It could mean saving thousands of innocent lives.

Archangel.

Something about the word still worried him, but he had no idea why. And that worried him all the more.

Archangel.

Damn it. Why did he feel so uncomfortable when he thought about that word? He couldn't help thinking that something was staring him right in the face, something important. But what was it? What was he missing?

He took a long, slow breath before finally making up his mind. Blake turned away from the screen, away from the endless ebb and flow of data, and addressed the oval panel on the wall to his left.

'Zen, how long would it take *Liberator* to reach the *Dionysus* platform on a direct course through the Cyrus Nebula, speed Standard by eight?'

Lights danced to and fro along the panel as Zen fed the information into the necessary systems. 'AT REQUESTED SPEED AND COURSE IT WOULD TAKE *LIBERATOR* PRECISELY 14 HOURS AND 32 MINUTES TO REACH THE LEISURE FACILITY KNOWN AS *DIONYSUS*.'

Jenna sighed. 'Is this really a good idea?'

'*Dionysus* is a refuge for every known dissident leader and political activist in the quadrant. In fact, it's the one place you can almost guarantee the Federation will be looking for us,' Avon said. 'So, why are we even taking the risk?'

'Because Vila's right, this could be a trap,' Blake said.

'Great. The one time someone listens to me and it's probably going to get us all killed,' Vila murmured, returning to the seating area. 'I wish I'd have kept my mouth shut now.'

'For once we agree on something.' Avon sounded pleasantly surprised.

Blake held his hands up, as though surrendering. 'We have to find out what Archangel is, Avon. We must know who or what we're up against, otherwise we'll just be stumbling blindly in the dark.'

'Isn't that our usual strategy?' said Avon.

Blake had to suppress the urge to laugh. He just couldn't win with Avon. Whatever course of action he took, whatever decision he made, in Avon's eyes it was always the wrong one.

'Correct me if I'm wrong but *you* brought this to *my* attention,' Blake said. 'What were you expecting me to do, just ignore it?'

'I was expecting you to listen to what the rest of us had to say for once,' said Avon. 'Or have you learned nothing from Gan's death?'

Avon turned away, not waiting to see the rebel leader's reaction.

'OK, I'll make you a deal,' Blake said, addressing his reply to the entire crew. 'Let me get in touch with Tobin first, on *Dionysus*. See how the land lies. Find out if he knows anything else about Archangel.'

'I don't know why we're even trusting him,' Vila said. 'He's a Federation officer.'

'An *ex*-Federation officer,' Blake reminded him. 'And a good man, who turned his back on the Federation several years ago. More importantly he's the co-ordinator for the Freedom Party on *Dionysus*. Which means he has access to a number of information channels outside of Orac's reach. And if he has any information for us, we'll sit down and decide together what the next step should be. We can even take a vote on what to do, if you like.' He spread his hands to show that he was sincere. 'If we decide that we don't want to take the risk, then we'll simply walk away and never talk of it again.'

Vila nodded his approval. 'Actually, I've always wanted to have a go in one of their hologram suites. We can make a sort of mini-break of it while we're there.'

'We'll be there for all of 30 minutes,' Blake said, smiling at Vila's disappointment. He turned to Jenna. 'What about you?'

'Forewarned is forearmed, I suppose,' Jenna said. 'So long as everyone else is in agreement, then it gets my vote.'

'Cally?' Blake glanced up at the communications module where the Auron sat, arms folded, watching her companions carefully.

'I think it makes sense to obtain as much information as we can before making a decision,' she said carefully. 'I am happy to go along with it.'

All Blake needed now was Avon's approval. Not that he *really* needed it; he had the rest of the crew's backing and was intending to go no matter what Avon said, but he'd rather have his colleague inside the tent spitting out, than outside the tent spitting in, as the old Amagon saying went.

Blake was sure that Avon knew everyone was waiting for him, that's why he remained silent. He wanted to make them sweat for a while, particularly Blake.

'Of course I'm in. I'm rather hurt that you should think differently,' Avon told him, with a smile. 'Besides, as you've already pointed out, it was me that brought this to your attention.'

He snatched up the operating key and the lights deep within Orac fell dark, the final whirr of power from his vacuum-sealed processors fading into gradual silence. 'Call Tobin and have him meet you on the platform,' Avon said. 'And if he has anything solid on what Archangel is, then we'll talk!'

artefact[1]

The girl ran as fast as she could.

She had no idea who she was or where she was going. She only knew that if she didn't get away from this place she was dead.

The corridor was slowly leading her upwards, towards the surface, of that much she was certain. If she could find a door, get outside, she might be able to hide from them, perhaps even find transport and get off this planet. It was doubtful, but it was the only shred of hope she had.

Above her, the ceiling lights spluttered alarmingly, the sporadic bursts of florescent light flashing through the darkness like summer lightning. She reached out until the tips of her fingers brushed the wall at her left side, then slowed her pace a little, feeling her way inch by inch along the corridor, waiting for the red emergency lighting to kick in.

In the near darkness she could hear them getting closer. The pounding of feet echoing towards her from somewhere further back in the direction of that cold, dark room she had left.

They were coming for her.

She'd hoped she would have more time before they discovered she was gone. Perhaps enough time to get clear, put some distance between herself and that room.

It had taken her a while to finally pluck up the courage. She'd even managed to stifle her screams as she'd unhooked herself from the instruments that were buried deep within her own body, pulling the wires and electrodes from out of her arms and legs and stomach… The one inside her head had been the worst; it had taken her nearly half an hour to pull that one free. The pain had been so bad she'd been unable to stop herself from crying out. Thankfully the room had been empty. Cold and dark and empty.

Except for the other six like her. Gabriel, Michael, Raphael, Uriel, Phanuel and Zarachiel…

The lights stopped flickering, plunging the corridor into total darkness, causing her to stop dead. She blinked her eyes, trying to dislodge the pale blobs that seemed to be burnt onto her retinas from the bright flashes of light, but it didn't help.

The girl staggered forward, beginning to panic now, both palms brushing against the cool metal surface of the wall as she tried desperately to put some distance between herself and the advancing footfalls.

There was something on the floor, something raised and solid. Her foot connected sharply with it and she fell headlong, fingernails clawing at the smooth wall, trying to find a handhold, anything to keep herself on her feet and moving away from her pursuers.

Disorientated, she began to drag herself along the floor on her hands and knees, one hand flailing in the air in front of her, terrified that at any moment her head might connect with something solid.

Desperately she tried to conjure a mental picture of the corridor, how it had been before the lights went out. There had been what looked like a maintenance shaft leading off to the right several metres ahead, and beyond that an opaque screen with a sensorpad entry system – probably a communications booth. And to her left there'd been…

Her heart began to pound as the image flashed into her head.

There *had* been a door, hadn't there?

She dragged herself to her feet, palms flat against the wall again, each foot now shuffling carefully in front of the other, warily testing the floor ahead for further obstacles. It had to be here somewhere. She was so sure that she'd seen it. She couldn't have been mistaken, could she?

Oh god, she hoped she was right.

Her fingertips found the outline of the door and she nearly cried out with joy, her eyes filling with grateful tears as she followed the groove that ran along the edge of the doorway. She stopped as her fingers brushed against the raised disc of the sensorpad, their tips dancing lightly over the eight tiny square keys at its centre.

She smiled to herself. She may not remember who she was or where she was being held, but she definitely knew the combination. She'd seen the man in white tap it into the dark room's sensorpad many times.

She reached out, carefully positioning her fingers over the appropriate keys.

Before she could press the final digit, the door rumbled open, catching the girl off-guard. She stumbled backwards, hands thrown up in front of her face, shielding her eyes from the glare. Someone was hovering on the threshold, a human-shaped hole cut into the light that shone from the room behind them. The figure stood there unmoving for a moment or two, before quickly swinging the barrel of a laser rifle around to cover her. It took aim.

'No. Not that way.' The voice came from further along the corridor, out of the darkness. 'I need her unharmed. Shoot her and the whole experiment becomes useless.'

The lights sprang on again, flooding the corridor in blinding white light, just as the trooper stepped forward. He spun the rifle around in his hands before the girl had time to react, smashing the shoulder-rest into her stomach, knocking the wind from her body. Then he reached down and grabbed her roughly by the arm, dragging her back along the corridor. Back to the dark room.

Sounds broke the darkness. Unrecognisable at first, then slowly they began to arrange themselves into familiar patterns.

'...rrnh..eernn..ing of test subject number six. After the first incision is made the neuron receptors will begin to fire. For this we will need the subject to be conscious.'

'But won't that be painful for the subject?'

'Yes, but not for long. 10 or 15 minutes, perhaps. Can't be helped, unfortunately.' The voice moved closer. 'If you can hear me I need you to open your eyes and look into the light beam.'

Her eyelids fluttered open. Light and shape and colour and memory bleeding slowly into the darkness, swallowing it up until everything became shades of grey.

'Good. That's it. You're doing very well. Now I need you to tell me your name. Not the name you had before, but the one now. Your *new* name. I need you to tell me your new name. Can you do that?'

She struggled to form the sounds, to eject them from between numb lips. She pushed hard but the sound was stuck somewhere at the back of her throat.

'Tala.'

It took her a few seconds to realise that she had spoken, that the voice she had heard was her own.

'No. Try again. Tala was your name before. What is your name now? Think.'

And suddenly the girl remembered it. 'Simiel. My name is Simiel, and I am the sixth of seven.'

'Good. Now we can begin.'

The girl who had once been known as Tala screamed as the fire tore through her body, flowing through her veins like molten lava, burning down her memories and turning them into thick, grey piles of ash.

Then slowly the darkness swallowed her up again, until there was nothing left but the cold and the dark and the unbearable pain.

CHAPTER TWO

Vila jabbed his second glass of adrenalin and soma in the direction of the main viewscreen. 'Is that it?' he asked, voice tinged with disappointment.

It had often been said that the *Dionysus* leisure platform was a thing of rare and magnificent beauty, a sight unmatched in the whole of the Caesari system. Granted, the people Vila had actually heard say it were members of the Terran Construction Cartel and, seeing as it was their company that built the thing, weren't exactly the most objective of sources. But even so, now that he was actually seeing the complex up close, he had to admit that he was far from impressed.

'Of course that's not it,' Orac snapped, its tone that of a weary schoolteacher talking to one of his less enlightened pupils. 'What you are seeing is merely the outer polyherculanium shell built to the Mark IV Bueller-Teshak civil administration platform specifications. I assume that what you are, in fact, interested in are the 1,950 fully-immersible hologram relaxation suites that are housed within and are said to be the most advanced and realistic of their kind.'

The news was like music to Vila's ears. Refilling his glass with a little more Soma he raised it in salute to Orac before taking a good, healthy gulp, then wiping his lips on the back of his hand. 'Well, that's more like it,' he said with a contented slur. 'I was beginning to think that we'd had a wasted journey for a minute.'

'It hardly matters one way or the other, seeing as you won't be going down there anyway.' Avon had appeared suddenly beside Vila's flight station, turning a data-cube thoughtfully over and over in his hands as he studied the giant structure on the screen.

'Actually no one will be going down, except me. ' Blake had his back to the rest of the flight deck, slowly strapping a gun-belt and power pack across his waist, before selecting a gun from the rack on the wall. He turned to face a row of silent, accusatory stares. 'We can't afford to take the risk. I've not made direct contact with Tobin for over a year, so I can't be completely sure where his loyalties lie at the moment. Until we're absolutely certain then I have to go down alone. It's imperative that *Liberator* remains safe at all times.'

'Another noble decision by our brave, self-sacrificing leader,' Avon noted, sardonically. 'So much for democracy.'

Blake said nothing for a moment, regarding his crewmate intently, then he shook his head. 'You would prefer a repeat of what happened at Central Control back on Earth?' he asked. 'Another one of us dead, like Gan? Perhaps a woman this time, just for balance?'

'That is hardly what I meant.' Avon turned slowly on the spot until he was looking Blake directly in the eyes. 'I don't understand why it has to be one extreme or the other with you. There are other choices besides going alone or getting us killed.'

Blake shrugged. 'Perhaps. But we've taken enough risks as it is lately.'

'No,' Avon interrupted. 'All the risks have been yours, Blake, not ours. Risks taken with our lives and with this ship. It's been the same ever since we stepped onboard. I'm only surprised that *more* of us haven't been killed.'

In response Blake flashed him a tight, humourless smile. 'All the more reason for me to go down there alone.' He clipped the gun firmly into its holster and checked the straps one last time. 'And if there are Federation troopers waiting for me, then you can always say you told me so. Although you'll have to say it very quickly and very loudly as I probably won't hear it over the sound of gunfire.'

It took a second or two for Blake's eyes to adjust to the subdued lighting of the main concourse, throwing him momentarily off balance. He staggered backwards a couple of paces, his shoulders connecting painfully with the main bulkhead.

There was a narrow corridor a few metres away from where he was standing, nothing more than a maintenance shaft really, that bisected the forward-most section of the *Dionysus*. There was barely enough room for one man to duck inside, let alone two, but it would have to do. Blake wandered casually along the far side of the concourse, his eyes on the flowing crowd of people that were unloading themselves noisily from the rank of civil transporter ships that sat in rows along the platform's expansive docking cradle. Choosing his moment carefully, he backed into the shadowy interior of the narrow shaft, and waited, one hand hovering over the butt of his gun.

Before long a tall man in sandy-coloured robes stepped out of the bustling throng of human traffic and shuffled quickly across the concourse towards Blake. He paused briefly at the mouth of the intersection, glancing back over his shoulder at the constant swirl and eddy of pleasure-seekers and freeloaders that filtered in through the main docking terminals, as though checking one last time that he had not been followed. Apparently satisfied, he covered the remaining distance in a brisk half-trot, the folds of his robes kicking up around his ankles like brown smoke.

The man squeezed himself into the cramped space beside Blake, lowering his hood to reveal a bald, glistening scalp. His large, dark eyes shone in the thick shadows of the maintenance shaft.

'Fleet Officer Tobin.' Blake relaxed a little at the sight of his old friend, a smile fluttering across his lips. 'I was starting to think you weren't coming.' He offered one hand to Tobin, who grasped it eagerly with both of his.

'Roj, good to see you again. It's been far too long, my friend, far too long,' Tobin told him, a fleck of sadness in his voice. 'I don't use that title any more. I tend not to dwell too long on my time in Space Command. It only serves to remind me that I have more years behind me than I have ahead.' And he ran the palm of one hand wistfully over the smooth, hairless dome of his head.

A cloud of exotic chatter swirled towards them from across the main concourse like a rising wind, dragging Blake back to the matter in hand. As much as the Caesari system liked to boast that it was neutral territory, the truth was there was very little they could do to stop Federation pursuit ships from patrolling through the area once every few days.

'I don't mean to seem rude, Tobin,' Blake said. 'But I need a little bit more information from you and I really can't afford to be here for long.'

'Of course. You must forgive me, my friend,' replied Tobin. 'Time is of the essence, I know.'

Tobin leant across and tapped an elaborate sequence of numbers and symbols into the tiny entrypad on the wall beside them. There was a sharp hiss of escaping air followed by a squeal of rusting hydraulics, and a small circular service hatch levered outwards, away from the wall. The freezing air hit Blake like a blow across the face. He'd forgotten just how cold it could get in the crawl-gantries that ran between the insulated interior spaces and the reinforced exterior skin of a space vessel.

From beneath his robe, Tobin produced a small, portable palmlight, which he kept switched off until he'd squeezed himself through the service hatch and was standing on the narrow, wire-mesh floor of the gantry beyond. He waited for Blake to climb through after him, then resealed the hatch and deactivated the entrypad.

They descended slowly through a series of inspection panels that led them deeper into the bowels of the leisure platform, the tunnels becoming narrower and narrower until, by the end, they were passing through crawl gantries designed to be used by the automated service robots. As they drew nearer to the section that housed the platform's orbital thruster array, the air began to prickle with an odd, semi-organic sort of drumming. To Blake, the accompanying electrical charge felt rather uncomfortably like an army of soldier ants swarming across his face and scalp.

A little further ahead, where the gantry was at its narrowest, Blake could just about make out the dark, oval smudge of an open doorway set into a shallow recess in the wall. Tobin ducked through first, quickly followed by Blake. Once they were inside, Tobin pulled a thin metallic data-key from the folds of his robes, and slotted it into a wall-mounted panel to one side of the door. He turned it smartly clockwise and the door snapped down into place, locking itself automatically.

After the bitter coldness of the long climb down, the air inside the ops-room seemed stifling and a little claustrophobic. The overhead lighting had been switched off and what little illumination there was came from a row of computer terminals and long range scanning equipment that dominated most of the back wall.

Tobin gestured towards the towering bank of active screens, inviting Blake to step further into the room and examine the technology for himself.

'I see the Freedom Party has been busy since I left Earth,' said Blake, a smile on his lips. 'I'm impressed.'

'We've had no choice,' Tobin explained. 'After the escape from Cygnus Alpha, the Federation started systematically tightening up its security procedures across the board.' He jerked his chin at the terminals in front of them. 'Without this, most of the Party would have been rounded up and shipped off to the alteration facilities on Pharrox months ago.'

Tobin ran a finger along a bank of red neon switches, slowly snapping each one into the *on* position. The equipment chattered into life, spewing out columns of non-linguistic data.

'We've been uplinked to the Federation archives for a while now, mostly fishing for encrypted files and military command reports, but this, well...' he paused. 'We've been trying to get our hands on information about Project Archangel for years. Anything we could find – documents, fleet reports, shipping manifests. But so far, it's all been rumours and hearsay. I wish I had better news for you, but...' Tobin shrugged, leaving the sentence hanging in the air, unfinished. 'That's why all I could give you was a name. You have to remember I was only a Fleet Officer, Blake. My security rating was strictly limited to Double-A clearance and below. And as far as I can tell, Archangel is off the scale.'

Blake studied him for a moment, then said, 'Meaning what exactly?'

'Meaning that this goes higher than I've ever known anything go. Whatever this thing is, it was buried a long time ago, and by the High Council themselves. I doubt that either Space Command or Servalan herself knows the full details.'

'You're telling me that absolutely no information either directly, or indirectly, linked to Archangel exists within the Federation computer archives?' Blake asked.

'Anything that was there has been removed.'

'So you have no information for me at all?' Blake asked.

Tobin shrugged. 'There are rumours.'

'I need solid facts, Tobin.'

'The thing about rumours, no matter how wild or fanciful, is that they are almost always based upon a single, irrefutable grain of truth,' Tobin said. He craned his head conspiratorially towards Blake, his eyes glittering in the artificial light from the computer terminals. 'Did I ever tell you about the time my fleet was stationed out along the borders of the Callidus system?'

It was meant as a rhetorical question. Blake knew this, so he remained silent, waiting for the ex-Fleet Officer to continue.

'This was before the colonial uprisings on the inner worlds three years ago, so most of the fleet was billeted to the Outposts along the Callidus border. At the time, the Federation were having a few problems with one of the ore-cracking stations out there. Some young hothead called Kaid was stirring up trouble. Threatening to blow the place sky-high with flutonic bombs unless the Federation withdrew its entire garrison. Something like that, anyway. Typical for those types of communities. So, naturally we'd all been shipped out there and placed on high alert. As it turned out, they didn't need us in the end. Kaid was killed by one of his own people and his body handed over to the Federation on the understanding that there would be no retaliation if they broke up the protests and returned to work immediately.

'I don't know if you've ever spent time in one of those Outposts – I'm guessing you haven't – but there's really not much to do except hang around the mess halls, play a few hands of Five-Card Jixx, or sleep. Well, I was in the Officers' Mess one day when I got talking to this pilot navigator called Roth, who confessed to me that he absolutely hated being out there – said the whole system gave him the creeps. An odd thing to say, don't you think? Not the Outpost, or the planet, but the whole *system* gave him the creeps. So, naturally, I asked him why. Do you know what he said?'

This time it was clear that Tobin was expecting an answer. Blake thought it over carefully for a moment then shook his head. 'Tell me.'

'He said the system was haunted. Can you believe that? He was serious too. Said he *knew* it was true because he'd seen things with his own eyes.'

'What sort of things?' Blake asked.

'Unexplained occurrences, Roth said. Like the sensors picking up ships that appeared from nowhere, then seconds later simply vanished.' Tobin clicked his fingers together. 'Just like that. When he tried to log the reports he was "advised" to forget what he'd seen. He said that *people* were disappearing too, along with any information about them on the computer systems. It was as if they had never existed. But I didn't really believe that, not straight away at least. Not until a few months later, when I was reassigned back to Earth. I got a vidcast from my wife, telling me that my son, Sheya, was missing. His ship had docked at the Outpost, but he wasn't on board. After that I checked every datafile I could lay my hands on, but I couldn't find even *one* mention of his name. It was as though he'd never existed.

'After that I decided to do some digging around, see what I could find on the Callidus system. I did it discreetly, of course. The last thing I wanted was a visit from the presidential guard in the middle of the night, and my body discovered a few days later with a laser bolt in the back of the head. I had to find my boy and I needed to be alive to do it.'

For a moment Blake wondered if that was how it had happened with his own family, if that was how his brother had died. Dragged from his bed in the dead of night and made to watch as they murdered his wife and son, before finally turning the gun on him. A shiver ran through him, despite the stifling heat of the ops-room. 'Very wise,' he said at last. 'Did you find him?'

Tobin shook his head sadly. 'The only thing I found out there were rumours. Mostly of an ultra-experimental new assault ship, a Stinger Class, that was supposedly being built out in the shipyards on Callidus IX. It was said to be capable of achieving speeds in excess of Time Distort 30.'

'Time Distort 30!' Blake repeated, genuinely shocked. He'd been prepared for a great many things, but this took him completely by surprise. 'But that's almost three times the speed of a regular Federation pursuit ship.'

'Yes, I know. There was a word connected with it too, something I heard from one of the Space Majors I talked to out there. He said that they were calling it Archangel.' Tobin shrugged. 'Though, as I say, it was just rumours.'

There was a pause as Blake considered the information. At last he said, 'Thank you, Tobin.'

Tobin shrugged as though he didn't really deserve it. 'I can't see how it will be much help to you.'

'It's a lead, at least,' said Blake. 'And that's all I can hope for right now.'

He turned to go, and Tobin put a hand out to stop him. Blake could see that his old friend seemed to be struggling with something, frowning as though he were unsure whether to speak up or not.

After a while Tobin shook his head, seemingly making up his

mind. 'Wait, there's more.'

Slowly he opened his fingers to reveal a small, black info-slug nestling in the palm of his hand. Light from the nearby computer terminal danced briefly across its tiny surface. 'This was smuggled out of the Braccus system aboard a civilian hospital ship a few days ago. It contains a single thread of data that the High Council appears to have overlooked. We didn't notice it at first, as it was practically undetectable on the initial system sweep, but once we'd run it through the encryption filters a few times we started to notice some faint ghosting, particularly on the earlier files. You need to see what we found.'

The info-slug wasn't strictly compatible with the equipment in the ops-room, so Tobin had been forced to improvise, modifying an old interface-patch from a Type 1 Federation pursuit ship. It wasn't perfect by any stretch of the imagination, but it did the job. Just about. He clicked the slug into place and a faint shimmering wisp of white smoke drifted up from the connecting lead. Almost immediately the computer terminals jerked into life, the data-stream a little slow at first as it struggled to cope with the erratic bursts of information that surged through the makeshift uplink.

Tobin cycled through an endless barrage of field reports and official communiqué, before stopping on a single page of information. It was a list of names. 'What you're looking at,' he explained, 'is a list of personnel – mostly scientific, but some military – who have, at one time or another in the last five years, been removed from various top-level projects without any explanations whatsoever, in most cases quite literally overnight. One day they're there, the next... gone. What is more, none of them have ever been seen or heard of again, although there is no record of their deaths either. All documentation pertaining to their reassignments has been erased from Central Archives. Each of those names have one thing in common – they are all linked to the secret Federation project codenamed Archangel.' He met Blake's gaze coolly and nodded towards the screen. 'Read the list, Blake.'

The list was mostly made up of names that Blake recognised – Doctors Bishov and Ardell of the Federation Space Drive Research Centre, the cyberneticist Keldo, and the neurosurgeon Pellas – but there were a handful that he'd never heard of at all such as the scientists Daines, Fredriks and Sylveste and the cybersurgeon Steinn.

Then he saw it.

At first it didn't register. The name was quite low down, somewhere near the bottom of the list, and his eyes skimmed across it without a second's hesitation. Then something clicked inside his head, causing him to stop dead. Slowly his eyes tracked back up the list until he found the name again.

Kodyn Tam – Cybernetic engineer, Grade 2/A.

His first thought was that it was a mistake, an administrative error, or a ghost thread from another file that had somehow become mixed up with this one. He looked up from the terminal screen, his eyes wide with astonishment. Then quickly, he reached for the teleport bracelet on his wrist, thumbed the communication button, and called the *Liberator.*

CHAPTER THREE

A flotilla of Federation pursuit ships were moving in at extreme sensor range by the time Blake arrived back on the *Liberator* flight deck.

Zen had been tracking them for several minutes and so far their course had remained unchanged; they were travelling at a steady speed along the edge of the system, probably nothing more than a standard patrol sweep.

'AT PRESENT SPEED AND COURSE, *LIBERATOR* WILL BE WITHIN SENSOR RANGE OF THE FEDERATION PURSUIT SHIPS IN 7.5 MINUTES.'

They broke orbit on the far side of the *Dionysus*, nudging the ship off at a discreet speed, trying their best not to attract attention to themselves. Slowly, the *Liberator* slipped away towards the asteroid belt, following a direct course out of the sector. All the time they were careful to keep the giant platform between themselves and the flotilla's sensors.

Blake waited until he was sure they'd shaken off the Federation ships before he told the others about the list Tobin had given him.

'You mean your old *friend*, Kodyn Tam?' Vila asked. 'The cybernetic engineer? The one who was killed five years ago?'

Avon peered sarcastically at Vila as he settled himself into the co-pilot module. 'As opposed to the *other* Kodyn Tam, equally famous throughout the Federation?'

Vila frowned in confusion.

Blake said, 'Yes, Vila. The one who died five years ago.'

Vila thought about this for a moment before answering.

'But he's dead, isn't he?' he said.

After that, the rest of the crew decided to leave him out of the conversation and he went back to flicking idly through his deck of cards.

Jenna switched through to autopilot and joined Blake by the seating area at the front of the flight deck. The ship was decelerating now as they reached the edges of the asteroid belt and Zen began to twitter impatiently, lights dancing in time as it awaited further instructions.

'Orac, I need you to scan the data stored on this device and transfer all information to the main screen.' Blake slipped a hand into the pocket of his tunic and pulled out the info-slug, cradling it in the palm of his hand. 'Then I want you to retrieve all available information on Kodyn Tam from Federation archives, with particular reference to the past five years. If he's alive then I want to know where he's been and what he's been doing.'

Orac huffed irritably, but complied none the less.

'And why hasn't he contacted you in that time?' Jenna was looking at the small, black slug that Blake had placed on the sensor plate near Orac, tiny power-lights blinking softly as the information was extracted.

Blake seemed to consider the question for a moment, before nodding towards the device. 'I'm hoping that Orac will find the answer in the archives.'

'Why are you assuming that Tam would have any desire to speak to Blake at all?' Avon spoke without looking up, continuing to examine the control panel in front of him.

His words caused Cally to suddenly stop what she was doing, her hand hovering in front of the console. 'He was Blake's friend. Why would he not want to speak to him?'

'Because it was due to Blake's negligence that Tam and his family were sent out of the Habitation Dome totally unprepared and completely vulnerable,' said Avon. 'Resulting in their capture.'

'I didn't know that they were unprepared,' Blake told him. 'He assured me he was ready to go. I thought I was doing the right thing.'

That made Avon smile. 'That's hardly the point. Even if he is alive, do you really think he has been enjoying the past few years? His wife was killed. His children were taken away from him. The fact of the matter is that without your interference, Blake, none of that would have happened.'

Blake said, 'Kodyn Tam came to me and asked for my help. He wanted to get away from the Earth and away from the Federation. He wanted his family to be safe. What was I supposed to do?'

They were interrupted by an abrupt electronic cough from Orac, as though it was trying to attract their attention.

'I have completed the requested tasks,' Orac announced somewhat pompously. 'The information is now available.'

'Let's hear it, Orac. Everything you've got,' Blake told the computer, though his eyes were still on Avon.

'Tam, Kodyn. Subject 405/64/2C. Third of four boys. Father: Rafen, Mother: Maree. Raised in the Tertian District of Habitation Dome Three until he was eleven years old, when his father…'

Blake flapped an impatient hand at Orac. 'Skip forward. Give me details from his supposed death onwards.'

'According to official Federation files, Tam and his family were caught attempting to pass sensitive documents to an unnamed terrorist cell working in the wastelands outside the Dome. They were arrested and found guilty of sympathising with known terrorists by a Federation court.'

'Two of those so-called "sympathisers" were his children,' Blake spat in disgust. 'The youngest girl was only eight.'

Orac continued, 'His wife, Lyssa, was killed while resisting arrest, and his daughters Katri and Tala were adopted by a family living in the outer colonies. Tam was later charged with four counts of terrorism and crimes against the Administration and executed three weeks after his arrest.'

'OK, we've heard what the official Federation files have to say,' Blake turned to look at the streams of data scrolling across the main viewscreen. 'Now let's hear the truth, shall we?'

The call came through five minutes after Blake had teleported back to the *Liberator*, just as Tobin knew it would.

He was sitting alone in the darkened ops-room when the communications console trilled lightly, the terminal to his left flashing up a *Call Waiting* notice in time with the sound. Tobin hesitated a moment, before leaning across and flicking the control to *Receive*.

A flimsy, holographic projection sprang up on the comms-panel in front of him, the ghost of interference across its skin dividing it momentarily into sparkling crystals of information.

'*It is done?*' The voice rattled through the tiny speaker-grill, prompting Tobin to quickly reach forward and turn down the volume.

Tobin nodded. 'I have given him the data-slug as you requested. Although what he will do with the information…' he shrugged, leaving the sentence to hang in the air.

'Blake will do what he always does.' The hologram shimmered briefly before returning to dark solidity. *'That is what I am counting on.'*

'Blake isn't stupid, you know,' Tobin hissed. 'He'll work out that he's being set up eventually.'

The hologram smiled, exposing a set of very white, very even teeth. *'And by that time it'll be too late, I'll have him exactly where I want him.'*

Tobin leant forward until his nose was mere inches away from the tiny hologram, blue-white light danced and rippled across his face. 'Then that is it, my part in all this is done.'

In reply the hologram shook its head. *'No, not yet. There's just one more thing that I need you to do.'*

'We had a deal,' Tobin hissed angrily. 'I pass the information onto Blake and his crew and in return you get my son out of Pharrox.'

'That is not quite how I remember it,' returned the hologram. *'I said if you did the things I asked of you then I would look into getting your son released. Pharrox operates a little differently to normal Federation prison facilities. Perhaps I don't have the authority that you think I do.'*

Tobin slammed his fist down angrily on the edge of the communications console. 'You're lying, that's not what you said. I've done everything that has been asked of me, I will do no more.'

'I want Blake!' the hologram shouted angrily, causing the speaker-grill to crackle with white noise. *'I want Blake and I want that ship. If I don't get what I want then neither do you, it's as simple as that!'*

He was trapped. Tobin knew it now.

At first he had believed that he could make this deal work for him, turn it around to his own advantage. And if he was clever he could use it to get back what the Federation had taken from him all those years ago – his son.

But at what price? He was betraying a friend, leading him to his death – or maybe something worse. Not only that, but he was condemning a lot of good people, too; people that actually mattered. The only people who had made any real difference since the colonial uprisings.

'They told me that you'd become obsessed with catching Blake,'

Tobin said. 'But I refused to listen. When I was a Federation officer, murdering scum like you would have been hounded out of Space Command.'

'*Probably, Tobin, probably.*' And the hologram nodded slowly, the anger now gone, replaced by the wide, shark-like smile once more. '*But that was such a long time ago, things have changed so much since your time.*'

There was a pause, and for a moment the projection rippled and wavered like a reflection cast across the surface of water.

'*Now, let's discuss this one last thing that I need you to do, shall we?*'

And for the sake of his son, Tobin knew he had no choice but to listen.

The data just didn't make sense.

Admittedly there were gaps in the information that Orac had managed to pull from the central archives. Most of it had been cobbled together from partially deleted files or ship manifests, but even so there was still nearly two years of Tam's life unaccounted for.

According to the unofficial records – files that were never meant to be seen by eyes outside of the Administration – Kodyn Tam had been taken to the holding facilities north of the Dome and held there for interrogation. Inquisitor Lerran had been assigned to do the actual interrogating, which probably meant that it had been quick and it had been painful.

Of all the interrogators and torturers working on Earth right now, no-one enjoyed their work with quite as much relish as Lerran, Blake thought, grimly.

Obviously Kodyn had told them what they wanted to know. It was inevitable really, once Lerran had become involved. He'd not told them everything, but what he had told them had been more than enough. Then he had disappeared. Vanished without a trace. Just like that. Nothing seen or heard of him for twenty long months.

Until he turned up in the prisoner lists on Sigma Minor.

So, he is alive, thought Blake. *Not even the Federation was stupid enough to dispose of a Grade 2/A cybernetic engineer. Someone of his skill, with his qualifications, would always be needed in some dark corner of the Federations oppressive regime.*

'Sigma Minor is supposed to be a *terrible* place,' Vila chipped in cheerfully. 'Full of subversives and deviants, sent there to have their brains altered by the best psychomanipulators in the business.'

Jenna shook her head. 'You're thinking of the alteration facilities on Pharrox.'

'No, Sigma Minor was first,' Vila said. 'Apparently they had to build the facilities on Pharrox to cope with the overflow from this place. That's what my old mentor Vorash told me, shortly before he was shipped out there.' He paused, considering this. 'Or *did* they send him to Pharrox?'

'It's a pity he wasn't sent there *before* he met you. At least then we'd have been spared his conspiratorial claptrap,' Avon said.

'Sigma Minor seems to have been Kodyn Tam's home for the past three years,' Blake said. 'Fortunately for us – and despite what Vila's friend may have believed – since the discovery of destrilium beneath its oceans ten years ago, it has operated as a joint labour camp and ore-cracking station, using the inmates as a slave labour workforce.'

'I suppose it keeps them out of trouble,' Avon said.

Vila was suddenly paying attention. Something in Blake's last statement had struck him as more than a little worrying. '"Fortunately for us"? Why "fortunately for us"?' he asked.

'Several years ago,' continued Blake, attempting to ignore the interruption, 'Sigma Minor was downgraded from a maximum-security facility and over 40 percent of its security forces were redeployed to other facilities. Presumably on the pretence that its inmates will be far too exhausted after a long day's undersea mining to even contemplate escape.'

'Why should it matter to us one way or the other what security arrangements Sigma Minor chooses to make?' asked Vila, his eyes wide.

'Unless I'm very much mistaken, we're about to make one of our famous rescue attempts,' said Avon, his eyes suddenly locking onto Blake's. 'Or am I misreading the situation?'

'As far as I'm concerned our deal still stands,' Blake told him. 'We do nothing unless we're all in agreement. But, let's just say that for the moment, I'm very interested in what happened to Kodyn Tam between his disappearance from Earth and his reappearance here. I would say it is almost certain that he was working on Project

Archangel. I would like to ask him in person. *Does* anyone have any objections?'

Up on the screen the scrolling column of data had wiped itself away, to be replaced by a grainy, 3D schematic that tumbled restlessly end over end.

'The layout is remarkably straightforward,' Blake said, 'with security being pretty much what you'd expect for a facility such as this – sensor pads, remote air cameras, parameter guard posts…'

Vila groaned. 'Listen to him, he talks as though we do this sort of thing on a daily basis.'

'We *do* do this sort of thing on a daily basis, Vila,' Cally replied.

'But nothing on this scale,' Vila argued. 'We're talking about a fully-armed, security-heavy prison complex. It'll be full of liars, cutthroats and murderers. And that's just the guards.'

'Look at it this way,' Avon said. 'This could be your big opportunity to die heroically for the cause.'

'Nobody's going to die, Avon. Not today,' Blake said. 'However, having said that, this complex does have one particular feature that gives me cause for concern. Orac, please relay all relevant data on Sigma Minor's energy barrier.'

'The energy barrier was initially designed by Emil Noon during his groundbreaking work on energy manipulation and how it can be applied to interstellar propulsion. He discovered that the gradual excitation of notronic particles formed a continuous, tight web of heavy…'

Vila held up his hand and silenced the computer. 'If we have to listen to this can we at least have it in a recognisable language? Or, failing that, in words that I can understand.'

'You may also want to use simple diagrams and illustrations,' Avon told the computer. 'Or, better still, glove puppets.'

'No, Vila's right,' Blake conceded. 'Skip the history, Orac. Let's just deal with how the barrier might affect us.'

Orac continued, 'Owing to the unique and *quite remarkable* nature of its structure, the energy barrier that surrounds the complex has a dual purpose. Not only is it designed to serve as a forcefield, similar in nature to the *Liberator*'s own force wall, but the formation of the molecular signature acts as a potent dampening field. While it is active, neither communication signals nor teleportation beams may pass through it.

'Unfortunately for us, the field is active pretty much all the time. It's only ever switched off when Civil Administration vessels land inside the complex.'

'And I'm guessing that there are none scheduled to make planetfall any time soon?' said Cally.

Blake shook his head. 'The last shipment of new prisoners was delivered there three days ago. A supply run isn't due for another three months.'

'So what are we meant to do?' asked Vila. 'Walk up to the front door and knock?'

This amused Blake. 'It's a nice idea, Vila, but I'm pleased to say we have something much better up our sleeves. Something that is unique to this ship, and can't be found anywhere else in the entire solar system. Something so brilliant that it is guaranteed to get us into that labour camp.' Blake pointed to Vila and then to Avon. 'We have the greatest lock picker in the quadrant and the most talented computer expert who ever lived. What more could we ask for?'

The laughter came as a surprise to Blake. It took him a moment or two to realise that it was coming from the direction of the co-pilot module and not from Vila's flight station.

'Your constant supply of optimism and sheer bloody-mindedness never ceases to amaze me, Blake,' Avon said. 'You really won't be happy until you've got every last one of us killed, will you?' The smile slipped quickly from his lips. 'Despite all your talk of democracy and letting everyone have their say, you really go out of your way to make it difficult for us to say no. One might even go so far as to say *impossible*.'

'Do I take it that's a no from you?' Blake asked.

The smile returned to Avon's lips, although it failed to reach his eyes. 'You know it's not, Blake.'

CHAPTER FOUR

A thin, cold mist was creeping in off the sea as Blake and Jenna teleported down to the planet's surface. Their forms had barely finished coalescing before they'd started to run the short distance across the sand towards a low collection of rocks.

Blake pulled a pair of binoculars out of his overcoat pocket and thumbed the power switch. With a hum, they sprang to life and he lifted them to his eyes, cycling through until the lenses were at full-magnification.

Through the sheet of hissing rain, Blake could just about make out the air-cams as they zoomed in and out of the perimeter line, scanning the surrounding area for thermo-heat signatures. Beyond that was a line of dark, low-roofed buildings that had been arranged to form a sort of cruciform shape. If Orac was right, these were the main detention cells and Kodyn Tam was in there somewhere. Although exactly where was anyone's guess.

With a sigh, he lowered the binoculars and handed them across to Jenna, pointing through the rain in the direction of the low-roofed buildings.

'If I'd have known the weather would be this nice, I'd have visited here a lot sooner,' said Blake, cuffing the rain from his eyes with the sleeve of his coat.

Jenna swept the binoculars slowly along the length of the perimeter fence, frowning as she thumbed the magnification controls. 'So far I've counted over half a dozen airborne cameras patrolling this side of the camp alone.' She lowered the binoculars and glanced across at Blake. 'Assuming there's a similar number stationed along each side of the camp perimeter...'

'Then we could be in trouble,' Blake nodded solemnly. 'All we can do is hope that Avon and Vila get their job done quickly.'

They kept themselves low as they broke cover, all the time keeping their eyes and weapons fixed on the perimeter fence. At the top of the ridge the beach ended abruptly, giving way to an uneven surface of cracked concrete slabs beyond. The thing had probably been a parade ground once, or a loading area for prison transporters, it was hard to tell. Either way, it was obvious that the area was now disused, bordered on all sides by thick tangles of wild grass.

Blake threw himself down into the grass, indicating for Jenna to do the same. He crawled forward on his stomach, moving with careful deliberation, until he reached the edge of the paved area. Slowly, he pulled the clumps of grass aside and peered through. From here he could see the side entrance to the camp along with the manned security checkpoint. Its barrier was just opening, allowing a squad vehicle through.

From the brief glimpse he'd got of the vehicle, as it had rumbled slowly forward and disappeared through the gateway, Blake estimated that there were at least two dozen troopers inside. Maybe more.

Blake activated the communicator on his bracelet, his voice barely above a whisper. 'Vila, this is Blake. Do you read me?'

After twenty seconds Blake tried again, but still there was no reply, only white noise.

The sun seemed always just about to set on Sigma Minor. That was one of the many things Vila hated about the planet. Trying to work in a state of perpetual twilight filled him with utter despair.

Although, if he was being honest, at this precise moment that particular irritant was slightly lower on the list than the one standing in front of him right now.

The thing Vila *really* hated about Sigma Minor was the heavily-armed Federation troopers that were trying to kill him.

The trooper was standing a few metres away by the door to the security station, his helmet tucked beneath his arm, the muzzle of his laser rifle pointing directly at Vila's heart.

'You must be wondering what I'm doing here,' Vila said, trying his best to sound casual. 'I'm a bit lost, you see. I'm trying to get to Capra Xindi but I think I must have taken a wrong turn at the Antaris Cluster.'

He realised that he still had his left boot in his hand and was waving it in the air as he spoke. He stood up, only to quickly sit back down again as his sock squelched in the muddy earth.

Unimpressed, the trooper took a step forward. 'Shed the weapon.' He indicated the ground in front of Vila. 'Throw it down there. Slowly.'

Reluctantly Vila did as he was told, sliding the gun from the belt and tossing it towards the trooper's feet, then he held up his hands to show that they were empty. Except for the boot, of course, he was still clutching that in his right hand.

'Do you mind if I put this on?' Vila waggled the boot. 'It's a bit on the chilly side down here and I think my foot's going numb.'

The trooper inched closer, towards the discarded weapon, all the time his eyes were on Vila

'As long as you keep your hands where I can see them, I don't really care whether you put it on or not.' The gun twitched as Vila's hands dropped. 'Nice and slow, now. You don't want me to get all edgy and accidentally put a bolt through your chest, do you?'

The trooper stopped as he reached the spot where Vila's gun lay, hesitating for a moment, before tossing his helmet to one side. Then he reached down. Fortunately for Vila, the trooper didn't see Avon until it was too late.

Avon dashed out of the trees, kicking the armed man just below the ribs, knocking him off balance. The Federation trooper rolled away, winded, the rifle flying from his hand and bouncing away into the undergrowth.

Avon lunged again, but this time the trooper was ready for him, ducking quickly beneath Avon's grasping hands. His body slammed against the ground, arm outstretched, as he reached for Vila's discarded gun.

In desperation, Avon swung a boot at the ground, hoping to kick the gun away, but he was too slow. The trooper snatched the gun up just in time, swinging it around towards his attacker.

Avon pushed himself forward, using his entire weight to catch the other man off-guard, groping blindly for the hand that clutched the weapon, struggling to keep the end of the barrel away from his body and out of harm's way.

Stars exploded across his vision as the trooper lashed out with his head, connecting sharply with Avon's nose, causing him to stagger backwards and his legs to buckle beneath him.

Then the trooper was on his feet and swinging the gun upwards, levelling it at Avon's head, squinting along the barrel as he took careful aim.

Avon closed his eyes and waited for death.

When it didn't come he opened his eyes again, just in time to see the Federation trooper collapse slowly to the ground, eyes wide with shock, mouth gaping in a silent scream.

Vila stepped away from the dead trooper, dropping the bloody knife as though it was white hot. 'Well don't just sit there,' he hissed, staring with distaste at the blood on his hand. 'Help me hide the body before we're discovered.'

Avon pulled himself painfully to his feet, snatching up Vila's gun on the way. 'Occasionally there are times when I'm almost glad to know you.' He thought about this for a moment, before handing the weapon across. 'Thankfully the feeling doesn't usually last for very long.'

They hid the body in the long grass, then clambered up over the rocks and down towards the rear of the security station, careful to keep out of sight of the air-cams that hummed noisily above the perimeter fence.

As they ducked out of sight behind an outcrop of rock, the bracelet on Vila's wrist trilled suddenly, causing him to almost yelp in surprise.

'*What's going on?*' Blake's hushed voice crackled from the tiny speaker. '*Why weren't you answering my call?*'

'We've been a bit busy.' Vila said. 'Avon's been making friends with the natives.'

'*Well get on with it.*' Blake was not amused. '*So far we've counted four patrol units in the area. Any more and that energy barrier will be the least of our worries.*'

Vila cut the connection as Avon scouted ahead, cautiously clambering down the rocks towards the edge of the perimeter. The area was clear. So far the dead security trooper had not been missed, although for how long it would remain this way he simply didn't know.

Avon signalled for Vila to follow him, then turned and headed for the open door of the security station. He paused on the threshold just long enough to check that Vila had started his descent down the rocks, before spinning on his heel and slipping quickly inside.

Base Camera Alpha 6 – Exercise Yard

A paved quadrangle in front of the main building. Two uniformed men walk by, both are armed, one wears a helmet but with the visor flipped up, the other is bareheaded. They stop briefly, exchanging a few words, then something is passed secretly from one to the other, something small, a piece of technology. It is slipped into a pocket, out of sight. The men go their separate ways.

CUT TO:

Base Camera Gamma 44 – Level Delta, Cells 25 – 40

Prisoners wander up and down, unhurried, oblivious of their surroundings. A uniformed man appears at the bottom of the screen. He stands half in and half out of the entrance to a cell. He backs up slowly, keeping his face towards the cell, looking into the open door.

Two guards drag a prisoner from the cell. The man is injured, beaten and bloody. He holds up his hands like he's surrendering. The first man steps forward, extending an arm towards the prisoner. In his hand he is holding a metal rod, forked at one end. He touches the prisoner with it and the picture flares, crackling briefly with interference, then clears. The prisoner screams, his body convulsing, twisting in agony, spittle frothing at the corners of his mouth and running down his chin in bloody rivulets.

CUT TO:

Remote Air Camera 012 – Perimeter Fence (South West)

A section of paved ground covered in grass and weeds. Beyond that is grey sand and ocean. There is a flash of movement at the edge of the beach: something is moving through the long grass. Then all is still again. A squad vehicle moves into shot, passing inches from the grass, blocking the patch of ground from view.

CUT TO:

The observation suite was surprisingly small, despite the amount of surveillance equipment and scanning tech that had been crammed in there. The main operations desk took up most of the space, positioned at the far end of the room, below a bank of infrared and thermo-heat monitors.

Avon waited for Vila to slide in through the half-open door, checked the corridor one last time – just in case someone had found the three dead security officers and raised the alarm – then sealed the door shut behind them.

Most of the lighting had been either turned down or off completely, giving the interior of the room a gloomy, somewhat muted tone. The only real light came from the instrument panels that littered the main desk, the rest from the bank of monitors on the wall.

Avon nodded towards the equipment. 'What are you waiting for, introductions?'

It wasn't exactly what Vila had been hoping for, but, as usual, he had to work with what he was given and was expected to perform miracles. 'Don't rush me. I'm thinking.'

'Is this really the time to be trying new things?' Avon asked.

Vila approached the operations desk like a concert pianist, hands raised, palms forward, wiggling his fingers to limber them up. 'OK, OK. Just give me a second or two. I need to familiarise myself with the equipment first.'

'Every minute we waste in here increases the chances of being discovered,' Avon said. 'Whatever you need to do, do it faster.'

Vila pulled an assortment of electronic key-cards out of his tunic pocket and began to steadily shuffle through them, as though he were about to deal himself a winning hand of Jixx. When he was satisfied with his chosen three key-cards, he set about feeding them into the card-drives on the main desk.

He waited until the constant thrum of the equipment became a steady, throbbing pulse, before pulling the electronic probe from his belt. He waved it towards the computer terminal.

'Alarm systems should be off-lining in a little under three minutes. After that the computer network is all yours.' He winked at Avon, a smile plastered across his face. 'I know what you're thinking, I'm a technical genius. You're right, of course, I can't deny it. It's a gift.'

Avon unbolted the maintenance cover on the terminal in front of him and began removing the memory circuits from the computer's motherboard, replacing them with the reprogrammed circuits he'd brought with him from the *Liberator*. When this was done, he thumbed the communication button on his bracelet.

'Blake, the computer network is rebooting. Surveillance systems will be down in approximately two minutes. Stand by.' He cut the connection then rechecked the progress of the network reboot. Once he was satisfied he turned to Vila. 'If we make it out of this alive remind me to give you a quick lesson on the virtues of modesty.'

A grainy holographic map of the interior of the labour camp flickered into life on the console in front of Cally, the image no bigger than her hand, shimmering in and out of focus as it spun lazily on the spot.

Cally glanced across at Orac, who sat on the table at the front of the flight deck. The supercomputer had been silent for a while now, ever since the others had teleported to the planet's surface, leaving it with a list of instructions.

He's probably sulking, Cally thought to herself.

It amused her to think that someone as brilliant as Professor Ensor would create a machine that was as emotionally unstable and unpredictable as a human such as... well, as Vila. It made absolutely no sense to her. To think that something with the ability to perform just about any task it was requested to undertake – and had access to almost limitless knowledge and information – had also been imbued with a temperament that often caused it to fly into fits of childish stubbornness and irrationality.

She shook her head and shifted her gaze back to the holographic map that continued to spin in front of her. Reaching across, she touched the image gently with the tip of her finger. It shuddered briefly, as though made of water, then it started to fold outwards like a flower opening its petals, eventually becoming an intricate, three-dimensional layout of the labour camp on the planet below.

It was the only map of the complex they'd been able to access. All the others had been either security encrypted or data-locked. In the end Orac had found a poor quality first-generation blueprint on a disused Federation computer network in the Ursinu system. The only trouble was it was incomplete – obviously created before the camp was redesigned to double as an ore-cracking station. Not only that but somewhere along the line the data had become corrupted and as a result the transmission just wasn't clear enough.

A wave of white noise rippled through the image and Cally tried switching off the power regulators, hoping the sudden electrical surge would clear the programme enough for her to extract the necessary information. At first nothing happened and she began to worry that the image might be lost altogether, but after a few seconds the rushing tide of static started to recede.

Cally tapped at the console, slowly sorting through the accompanying data as it flittered across the screen, cross-referencing it with the broken and incomplete pieces of information that littered the holographic map.

After a moment Zen began to twitter, lights flashing urgently in time. Cally raised an eyebrow in response, only half-acknowledging the computer's presence.

'INFORMATION: LONG RANGE SENSORS DETECT FEDERATION PURSUIT SHIPS ON AN INTERCEPT COURSE WITH *LIBERATOR*, BEARING THREE-FOUR-TWO, MARK ONE-SEVEN.'

Slowly Cally looked up from the computer screen, her face pale, eyes wide with shock. Without thinking, she reached over and jabbed the communicator controls to warn her friends.

It took Blake three attempts to prime the explosives. It wasn't so much that he was afraid they were going to explode in his hand (although there was always that worry, particularly as he'd not used this type of explosives before) more that the constant curtain of misty rain was coating his hands, making the delicate work of wiring in the primers very tricky.

Not to mention dangerous.

With a sigh of relief, Blake snapped closed the casing of an explosive charge and placed it on the ground with the others, then reached into the front pocket of his holdall for the last one.

Jenna pushed her way through the grass and hunkered down next to Blake, scooping the explosives up carefully, one by one, and placing them back into the holdall, out of the rain. The last one she held on to, weighing it thoughtfully in her hand as she waited for the guards standing at the side gate to move a little closer. She twisted the small metal cap at the top of the explosive then yanked it free, taking careful aim.

At first nothing happened. She had counted to six before throwing it towards the target, just as Avon had instructed. It had landed exactly where she had intended it to, by the door of the sentry station. But so far there had been no explosion.

Blake raised his head above the waving line of grass and peered towards the side gate. He could see the explosive lying on the paved ground, a metre or so from the door of the sentry station. One of the gate troopers, a short stocky sergeant, was scowling suspiciously, not quite knowing what to make of it. He swung the rifle from his shoulder and began to approach the object cautiously.

The explosion lifted the man off his feet, pitching him head first into the metal gate some 30 metres away, the impact snapping his neck, killing him instantly. The other trooper was dazed. The blast had ripped the helmet from his head and cut his forehead pretty badly, the blood running in deep rivulets down his face.

Jenna twisted the cap off a second explosive device and tossed it in the same direction as the first. This time the explosion came on the count of ten as it was supposed to, ripping the side gate from its hinges and filling the air with a noxious cloud of sooty ash.

Through the now open gateway, Blake could see the first of the squad units emerging from the buildings beyond. There were twenty or thirty men in total, although Blake knew that this was only the beginning. More would come soon, many more, not only from inside the complex but also from the direction of the spaceport. There'd be armoured vehicles too, eventually. That's when it'd get *really* tough.

'Here they come!' Blake shouted, and carefully aimed his gun at the approaching troopers, at the same moment the communicator on his wrist started to beep.

Beside him Jenna drew her gun and quickly chose her first target.

artefact[2]

It was the first time that he had seen what he looked like.

Not that he had any real memory of his life before, that had been taken from him months ago – all traces of his life flushed away, not just from his own mind but from the Federation banking system, the computer archives, Central Records, everywhere.

Nothing left.

It was easy enough to do, if you had the right piece of technology. They'd released a dataworm into the system, that's what Keldo had told him not long after the first phase of implants, when the pain was finally subsiding.

'It's not really a worm, of course. At least, not in a real sense.' The cyberneticist had been standing by his Cradle, adjusting the nutrient-feed that was attached to the vein in his arm. 'It's a sentient viral strain that is programmed to work its way through the information systems and eat away all traces of… well, whatever it's been programmed to eat away at. In this case your biodata.' Keldo stopped, glancing sideways at him. 'It doesn't really eat the data, of course. At least, not in a real sense.'

After that, he'd heard very little else of what the cyberneticist had said, the sedatives were starting to wear off and the dull throb of pain was returning. Very soon it would blot out everything.

There was no sense of time in this place, not any more, not since the experiments had begun; but he knew that he must have been here for quite some time. It was the Cradle, it had a way of altering your memories, distorting your perception of the passage of time, until time seemed to bleed into itself and one day was exactly like the next.

And so he found himself sitting in the operating room one morning, without any recollection of how he'd got there, looking at himself in a mirror for the first time. The metal table was cold beneath his bare buttocks and the patches of skin on his extremities, chest and forehead, where the wires of the Cradle penetrated his body, suspending him from the lab ceiling, were itching like mad. From the corner of his eye he could see Keldo watching him, ready to step in the moment he saw any signs of a mental shutdown.

Sometimes it was a shock for them, particularly after the extreme isolation of the Cradle Room, Keldo had told him. So far he'd had to deal with three such cases – the two girls and the pilot. Which effectively meant starting again from scratch with them – memory wipes, the lot. To tell the truth, he'd had serious misgivings about allowing Subject Four the mirror this early into the tests, but it was out of his hands. The Project Director had insisted.

'This is you, Zarachiel,' Keldo said cheerfully. 'Your new self. Or, rather, the *road* to your new self – we're far from finished yet.'

The man who was now called Zarachiel put a tentative hand to his face and trailed the tips of his fingers along the fusion of skin and metal that criss-crossed his face.

Keldo nodded encouragingly. 'The implants have taken nicely, I'm really rather pleased with them. They may be a little red and sore at the moment but that's normal for this type of procedure. You'll get used to it, in time.'

The man said nothing for quite some time, continuing to stare at his own reflection. After a while he reached forward and gently plucked the mirror from the cyberneticist's hand, turning the reflective glass this way and that, as though he were admiring the man's handiwork.

At first his face was blank, totally expressionless, as he regarded the horrific image that stared back at him, slate-grey eyes almost black in the harsh lighting of the overhead sensorlamps. Then a shadow passed over Zarachiel's face; something new, something that Keldo had never seen before, and instinctively the cyberneticist reached for the panic button.

It was too late. Zarachiel's fingers were no longer caressing the reddened flesh. He had worked his long fingernails into the joins, where fused skin met metal implant, and was pulling the two apart. There was a soft, wet ripping sound and Zarachiel began to scream as his flesh tore, yellowy-red pus spilling from the hole as the plate ripped away from muscle and bone.

When the orderlies arrived they halted inside the doorway, unable to move, staring in horror at the man's bloody body. Keldo shouted for them to restrain the test subject and they quickly darted forward, grabbing at the man's wrists, forcing them down by his sides. His hands were clenched like talons, clawing fiercely at the air in front of him, glistening red strips of skin hanging from beneath his fingernails.

By the time they had managed to sedate him and strap him down onto a medical trolley, he had torn most of the new implants free from his chest and neck. His face was almost unrecognisable, the skin and muscle obliterated, his left eye hanging down from its socket on a thin, sinewy cord.

'Is he beyond repair, or can we still salvage something from the wreckage?'

Keldo peered through the glass at the bloody mess lying on the operating table and sighed. 'With all due respect, Director, this is a human being we're talking about. We won't know whether we can repair the implants until his condition stabilises.' He took a deep breath, then added, '*If* it stabilises. The damage he inflicted upon himself was quite extensive.'

'So I gather.' The Project Director really didn't sound pleased. 'This time the implants were torn out right in front of you and still you failed to stop it happening.'

Keldo turned and stared into the darkness, towards the direction of the Director's voice. 'I did everything I could, under the circumstances.' He shook an accusatory finger. 'I warned you that Subject Four was not ready for this, his mental state was far too fragile. It was exactly the same with the other three. You were sent all my reports along with Neumann's psych evaluations. Our findings were plain enough. We didn't give them enough time to adapt. You have to understand it's not only the physical trauma our test subjects have to deal with, but also a massive mental upheaval. Most of them don't even have the capacity to –'

'This is the fourth such incident in as many months,' the Director snapped, cutting him off. 'I want steps taken to see that this never happens again.'

'But that's what I'm trying to tell you,' Keldo said. 'There's nothing we *can* do about it. We cannot hasten along a human's mental state any more than we can push the moon out of its orbit with a single pursuit ship. It's impossible. The test subjects will be ready when they're ready, simple as that.'

There was a faint squeal of metal, followed by the rustle of heavy fabric, as the Director stood and strode across the room towards the cyberneticist. 'Time is the one luxury that we cannot afford, Keldo. The High Council is already demanding results. I need something I can show them, something solid, something positive.'

'What about the propulsion tests? Pellas tells me that the craft refits are almost complete.' Keldo tried to sound optimistic. 'Perhaps Bishov or Ardell could speak with the High Council, show them the extent of their work?' He spread his hands. 'It might placate them a little, give us more time to perfect the grafting procedure.'

The Director stepped closer to the glass and gazed into the darkened room beyond. 'The High Council is not concerned about the Stingers. They saw the working prototypes for those a long time ago. No, it is *this*,' and the Project Director tapped a fingernail lightly on the glass, 'that is making them nervous. Unless we can present something to them soon they will get cold feet and shelve the entire project. They are close to it already.'

They fell silent for a moment or two, watching the masked figure in the other room intently as he probed the test subject's self-inflicted wounds. When the examinations were complete, he straightened and turned to face the glass partition. He shook his head solemnly, before dropping the bloody scalpel into a nearby sterilising dish.

The Project Director turned away from the scene, back pressed against the glass, and sighed. 'You'll need a new test subject to replace him, preferably another male.' The Director smiled. 'I think I have the ideal candidate in mind. I'll have him relieved of his duties and shipped out here immediately.'

Keldo nodded. 'I also require another mutoid. If we are to start from scratch I'll need more tissue samples. All the others have atrophied. We're finding it difficult to keep vampire meat fresh for longer than three days.'

The Director pushed herself away from the partition and moved across the room towards the door. Keldo watched her go, finding it almost impossible to drag his eyes away from her retreating form.

'Remember, the High Council is demanding results.' She stopped and turned, flashing him a smile. 'You've always been my favourite, Keldo. I know you won't let me down.'

The cyberneticist's mouth twitched momentarily as the implication of her words suddenly struck him. He bobbed his head in a curt nod. 'Yes, Director Servalan.'

He continued to watch her as she slipped from the room, the door sliding shut behind her with a *shush* of hydraulics. Then she was gone.

Only then did Keldo allow himself to relax.

CHAPTER FIVE

When the energy barrier finally came down Vila was just as surprised as anyone else in the complex.

He rechecked the instrument panel, just in case he'd made a mistake. No, there it was: power levels were at 48 percent and dropping rapidly. The energy barrier was slowly cycling down.

'Hey, I've done it!' He glanced up at the wall of monitors; most of them were either dark or fizzing with grey static, the rest were having trouble focusing. It wouldn't be long before they were non-operational like the others.

Vila swung round, waving the electronic probe in the direction of the dead monitors. 'I've done it!' he repeated.

'I think you'll find that I helped a little,' Avon told him, snapping the maintenance cover back on to the terminal, then scooping up the extracted memory circuits and stuffing them into his pockets. He set the controls on his teleport bracelet to multi-channel, before clicking the communication button. 'Blake, Cally, it's done! The barrier is down. We need those co-ordinates, *now!*'

It was taking too long. Orac really should have finished by now.

Cally drummed her fingers impatiently on the teleport control console and checked the ship's clock for what felt like the hundredth time. It had been nearly two minutes since Avon's call and she knew that it wouldn't be long before he contacted the ship again, this time sounding a little more desperate. They had done their job – well, the first bit of it, anyway – by getting the barrier down, and now the continued success of this mission depended on whether Cally could get them out of the security station and into the correct cellblock – or as close to it as possible.

She glared across at Orac, unable to keep silent any longer. 'Time is running out, I need those calculations now. Avon and Vila are counting on me.'

'I must familiarise myself with the complete layout of the labour camp if I am to extrapolate the optimum co-ordinates for teleportation,' Orac snapped back. 'The tiniest error in my calculations, even the smallest decimal point in the wrong place, and there is every danger that their molecules could reassemble inside a solid object. Which is more preferable to you, that I do this quickly or accurately?'

'Right now, I'd rather have both,' she said.

'That was not an option,' Orac retorted testily. 'Therefore your answer is not only irrelevant, but also somewhat lacking in intelligence.'

Cally glanced up at the clock again, her fingers hovering over the teleport controls. 'I'll give you one more minute, Orac, and if you don't have the co-ordinates for me by then I'm bringing everyone back up to the ship.'

'That will not be necessary. I have finished my calculations and am transferring them to your console now.' There was an air of smugness in the computer's voice. 'All that was needed was a little patience. You might want to consider this the next time you are in a similar situation.'

But Cally was no longer listening. With one hand she had activated the communicator, setting the signal to multi-channel transmission, with the other she was powering up the teleport controls, waiting for the directional guidance computer to lock on to the Orac's co-ordinates – the general location of Kodyn Tam's holding cell.

'Blake, Avon, stand by. Teleporting now!'

Cally flicked the controls and the teleport chamber sprang into immediate life. She reached across and operated the booster circuits, snapping down each of the three levers, allowing the power to build steadily as she attempted to teleport four separate molecular patterns to two places – Avon and Vila over to the holding cell, Blake and Jenna back to the Liberator.

Even though they'd never tried it before, Orac had assured her it would work, reluctantly taking her through the process step by step. As long as she stuck to his instructions precisely, both parties down on the surface of the planet could, theoretically, be teleported successfully at the same time.

The inside of the teleport chamber had begun to shimmer with a strange light. Patterns of energy and colour danced sporadically through the air, slowly coalescing until a vaguely humanoid figure was discernible. The humanoid figure split into two, quickly becoming more defined, until both were surrounded by a crackling halo of light.

Abruptly the pulsing stopped and the now-solid forms of Blake and Jenna stepped hastily from the teleport chamber.

Blake patted himself down, as if to make sure that all his limbs were still intact and in the right places. 'Now that was an interesting experience.'

'Not one I'd like to repeat again any time soon,' Jenna agreed.

According to the system log, the simultaneous teleport had been a success, just as Orac had predicted, but, even so, Cally waited for Avon to call in and confirm before she shut down the teleport controls.

Orac's co-ordinates placed Kodyn Tam's position at the tip of the north spike in the cruciform-shaped building, over on the east side of the camp. Cally opened up the holographic map and waited until it slowly unfolded itself, then zoomed in on the appropriate section.

She'd managed to sharpen the image slightly, which meant the magnification of the map could be increased by roughly 50 percent. Yet despite this, Blake still had to crane his head forward in order to study the layout properly. He carefully spun the image around so that he was now looking at the detention blocks from the northeast corner.

'I want you to put me back down here.' Blake indicated a small, paved walkway that ran the length of the block. 'Just a little to the west of where Avon and Vila teleported.'

The news took Cally by surprise. 'You're going back down there?'

Blake unclipped his gun-belt then quickly shed his rain-sodden topcoat, exchanging it for the dry one that Cally had retrieved for him from one of the equipment lockers. It was cold and damp on the surface and the last thing he needed was his hand shaking from the chill as he aimed his weapon.

'Avon and Vila could be walking into trouble. They might need my help,' Blake said.

'I'm sure Avon knows what he's doing,' Jenna said, running her fingers through her damp hair.

'It's not Avon that I'm worried about.' Blake headed back towards the teleport chamber, snatching up the gun-belt on his way over, and fixing it back around his waist. He turned and drew his gun from its holster, then nodded his readiness. 'Twenty minutes. If you've not heard from us by then, turn the ship around and get the hell out of here.'

Cally powered up the teleport controls once more, quickly keying in the new co-ordinates before switching the console over to *transmit* mode. The lights inside the chamber began to pulse, and in the next moment Blake was gone.

'How long until the pursuit ships move into intercept range?' Jenna asked, stripping herself of both gun-belt and teleport bracelet.

'If they remain at their present speed, about 32 minutes.' Cally told her.

Jenna nodded. 'It's tight, but it should still give them enough time.' She looked uncertain, half-convinced.

'Assuming no more Federation ships turn up,' Cally said grimly. 'Then we really *are* in trouble.'

'We'll worry about that if and when it happens.' And with that Jenna turned on her heel and headed for the flight deck.

Vila hated prisons. They reminded him of his childhood – and that was one period in his life he'd really prefer to forget.

They were in the prison yard in front of the detention block. To their right they could just make out the vast steel tripods of the ore mines further along the coast; to their left, great plumes of slate-grey smoke hung in the air above the westerly perimeter fence, the welcome result of Blake and Jenna's diversion.

The block's main security door was still standing open, the interior of the building beyond was dark and unnaturally silent; to Vila it looked alarmingly like a large hungry animal with its mouth open, patiently waiting for them to approach.

They scuttled across the yard, keeping their backs close to the wall. On the ground just in front of the security door an air-cam was lying on its side, flopping listlessly to and fro like a fish out of water. Avon prodded at the machine with the toe of his boot and it gurgled somewhat pathetically in response. He crouched down and examined the device a little more closely.

'It's resetting its programme parameters,' Avon said. 'Trying to re-establish a connection with the computer core.'

Vila looked down at the machine with something resembling pity, as though it was a wounded animal. 'Can it do that?'

'Not while the computer is rebooting. But once the main power systems come back online it might just be able to link up again.' Avon pulled himself to his feet and immediately started towards the open security door.

Inside the building seemed dark and deserted, their footfalls echoing eerily up and down the corridors as they raced towards the stairwell that would take them down to the lower detention levels.

Avon stopped at the foot of metal stairwell, slowly spinning around on the spot, checking that they weren't being followed. In his haste, Vila almost fell the last few steps, grabbing hold of the handrail at the last moment and struggling to keep himself vertical.

'I don't like this, it's too quiet. It's not normal,' Vila hissed, glancing nervously into the shadow-drenched corners.

At first Avon didn't reply. He was still turning slowly on his heel, his head angled slightly to one side, eyes narrowed, as though he was trying to hear something that was just beyond his range.

After a while he said, 'Something's wrong. Even with Blake's distraction at the side gate there should still be a handful of guards. Unless they're...'

'Drop the guns and let's see those hands!'

Vila heard the sound of laser rifles being cocked and knew they'd walked straight into an ambush.

There were three men altogether; they were on the floor above and making for the stairwell. Two of them were wearing riot-helmets while the third was in a sky-blue boiler suit, a faded prison logo stencilled on his left breast pocket. This last one wasn't a Federation guard like the other two, Vila realised with distaste. He was a trustee.

One of the prisoners.

'You heard me, lose the weapons.' They'd reached the top of the steps now and the trooper at the front jabbed the muzzle of his rifle at the two rebels. 'I won't tell you again. Next time it'll be a bolt through the head.'

Vila didn't need any more prompting. He detached his gun from its power-lead and tossed it away. The weapon went skittering into the shadows as Vila raised his hands, eager to show that he was completely unarmed and no longer a threat.

The trooper's rifle tracked slowly away from Vila, finally coming to rest on Avon. 'What about you? Are you going to be a good little rebel too, like your friend here, or are you planning on playing the hero?' Then he smiled. It was a smile, Vila noted, that didn't quite reach his eyes.

The gunshot seemed to come from nowhere, echoing down through the deserted detention block and rebounding off the high metal walls. The trooper at the back pitched forward, hitting the railing with his chest, causing him to crumple slowly to the floor.

Instinctively, Avon dropped down onto one knee, raising his gun in both hands. He took careful aim and pulled the trigger. The bolt caught the second trooper squarely in the chest, flinging him backwards up the stairwell.

This just left the trustee standing alone at the top of the steps, rifle hanging limply in his hands, as he stared between Avon and the direction of the other gunshot. Eventually he dropped the weapon, letting it clatter end-over-end down the steps, where Vila scooped it up.

'Next time don't leave it so long,' Avon shouted into the gloom at the top of the stairwell.

Blake stepped from the shadows, gun raised to cover the now unarmed prisoner. He stopped at the top of the steps. 'A "thank you" is usually customary in these situations.'

'Thank you. Only next time don't leave it so long,' said Avon.

As the three men were conversing, the trustee began to shuffle slowly backwards, heading for the open security door behind him, hoping to escape to the upper levels. He stopped suddenly as Blake turned to look at him, thrusting his hands even higher into the air as if to prove that he wasn't doing anything untoward.

'These clothes...' Blake said, indicating the faded white crest on the front pocket of the man's overalls. 'They're prison issue. You're a prisoner, yes?'

The man nodded, keen to show them that he was being cooperative. 'Yeah... I mean, yes. They're for the Blue Grades. I'm a Blue.'

'Blue Grade?'

The prisoner stared at him, seemingly confused that he had to explain. 'It means I've kept my nose clean since I was brought here. Not caused any trouble. So they upgraded me to a Blue. I'm a trustee.'

'And what is it that you trustees do, exactly?' Avon asked, with some bitterness. 'Apart from helping Federation guards terrorise the other inmates.'

The prisoner continued to stare at Blake, unblinking, making a show of ignoring the other man's question. After a few seconds he dropped his eyes and whispered, 'In here we all do what we can to survive. You wouldn't understand.'

Blake smiled tightly, his voice becoming a little friendlier. 'You'd be surprised. We understand more than you think,' he said. 'What's your name?'

'Tymon.'

'Listen, Tymon, we need to find a man called Tam. Kodyn Tam. He's being held on Level Delta, Cell 35. We need you show us the way,' Blake said. 'It's very important to us.'

'You're Blake, aren't you? The one that escaped from Cygnus Alpha.'

'Yes,' Blake told him.

A slow smile spread over Tymon's face. Then he walked past Blake, stopping as he reached the top of the stairwell and glancing briefly at the two rebels on the lower floor. 'Level Delta isn't down that way, you've come too far.' He jerked his chin back towards the open security door that led to the upper levels. 'Come with me, I'll take you the quick way. The way that only the prison guards are supposed to know about.'

Corridors and passageways flashed by the four men as they tore from the observation gantry and plunged into the bright honeycomb-like tunnels of Level Delta, the sound of gunfire pounding all around them.

They'd forgotten about the cell doors; it hadn't crossed their minds that the power-outage would have automatically sealed them all. In the event of a power loss their default setting was diametrically opposite to the security doors, thus designed to keep the prisoners safely locked in while not trapping the guards inside the main detention area.

Now they had no choice but to dig in and keep the pursuing

troopers out there on the gantries and away from the cells while they waited for the system to finish rebooting and come back online.

'The main system is designed to cycle up in a particular sequence.' Avon explained, wincing as a shower of sparks erupted above his head. He slid himself further down behind the makeshift barricade before continuing. 'Lights, doors and lifts first, followed by surveillance and tracking, then communication and energy barrier. The idea is to allow enough time for the generators to power up sufficiently to feed the more energy consumptive systems, otherwise the whole thing will trip again.'

Despite his best efforts, Blake was finding it difficult to get his head up far enough over the top of the barricade to be able to see the troopers clearly. By his reckoning there were at least a dozen armed men stationed along the top of the gantry, maybe more. It was difficult to know for certain. He poked the barrel of his gun over the top of the upended table and loosed a volley of shots in the direction of the troopers, but most of them went wide of the mark, rebounding harmlessly off the metal guardrail.

But where the hell had they come from? One minute the hallway had been clear, the next... It was almost as if the troopers had been up there waiting for them.

He settled back down behind the table and checked the power pack on his belt. It was half empty. 'How long after the doors become operational will the barrier be up and running again?'

'Hard to say.' Avon was waiting for the barrage of gunfire to ease off long enough for him to get a shot in. 'Assuming the generator is one of the old mark-threes, the power cells will need to recharge a little first.' Then he was on his feet, firing off three clear shots before he was driven back down again by another explosion of sparks. 'Eight minutes. Maybe more, if we're lucky.'

'That's always assuming that those pursuit ships haven't reached planetary orbit before then,' said Blake.

Vila had wedged himself tightly in the corner, his knees pulled up against his chest, hands covering his head. He looked up briefly as the thick metal table shuddered violently against the impact of a volley of rifle shots. 'I want to change my vote. I don't think we should have come here after all. Who cares what Archangel is? I'm sure it's not that bad. Let's leave them to it, that's what I say!'

The overhead lights suddenly flickered on, illuminating the entire stretch of corridor as far back as the detention cells, causing Vila to yelp in surprise and bury his head in his hands once more. But then hands were grabbing at him, yanking at the collar of his tunic, dragging him to his feet by the scruff of his neck.

'Get on your feet, Vila, now!' Blake shouted at him.

By the time they had reached the row of detention cells, power was bleeding steadily back into the system. The line of terminals at the far end of the corridor sprang to life. At first they were a broken mess of white static, then each screen began to clear as the computer circuit started its automatic reloading procedure.

Tymon stopped suddenly, pointing towards the far end of the line of prison cells. 'Each row contains roughly fifteen cells. You will find number 35 back that way, further along the gantry. The doors are operated through a central locking mechanism that runs through each section.'

There was an explosion in the direction of the barricade, followed by the sound of gunfire. The troopers were through. They would be there in a matter of minutes.

The four men turned and fled in the direction of cell 35, frantically searching for anything that they could use to block the corridors, to slow the advance of the security troopers. But there was nothing.

They sealed the security door behind them and Vila quickly pulled the electronic probe from beneath his tunic, using it to short out the entrypad mechanism. It wouldn't hold them for long, but it would allow them a little more time.

Cell 35 was the fifth door along. Blake skidded to a halt in front of the closed hexagonal portal and peered in through the tiny plexiglass window set into a small recess at head height. Although it was still dark inside the cell, he could just make out the shadowy form of someone slumped across the hard, one-man bunk that jutted from the rear wall of the cell.

From further along the corridor came a strange ululating whine, followed by the crackling hiss of reinforced metal liquefying under extreme temperatures.

Avon threw himself against the wall, sliding slowly and carefully towards the edge, peering around the bend in the corridor. Sparks spewed from the surface of the sealed security door. A glowing finger of light traced a thin white-hot circle about a metre or so from the lip of the door, where the metal was at its thinnest.

'They're cutting through!' Avon shouted over his shoulder. 'If you're intending to get him out of that cell, Blake, then now would be a very good time.'

Blake jerked his gaze away from the interior of the cell and glanced down at Vila. 'Come on, Vila, we're running out of time!'

The thief was on his knees, jabbing at the guts of the lock with his electronic probe. Bits of the mechanism were spread out on the floor around him like tiny orbiting moons and satellites. 'Why is everyone always trying to rush me? I'm going as fast as I can.'

'I thought you were supposed to be the quickest thief in the five galaxies,' Blake said. 'At least, that's what you're always telling us.'

'I said I was the *best*! The *best* thief in the five galaxies, not the fastest!'

'Well right now you need to be both!' Avon shouted at him from further down the corridor. 'In two minutes they're going to be through that security door.'

Tymon pointed at the rifle slung across Vila's shoulder. 'If you were to give me back my weapon I could help keep the troopers busy for a while, give you time to work on the lock.' He shrugged as though he didn't really care what happened one way or the other. 'It's up to you, of course. Though it looks to me as if you could use all the help you can get.'

Blake thought about it for a moment, before nodding. He had no real reason to trust the man, but time was against them and he didn't feel that he could afford to turn down the offer of help, no matter where it came from.

He unhooked the gun from Vila's shoulder and tossed it across to Tymon, who immediately checked how much charge was left in the power pack. Apparently satisfied, Tymon snapped the pack back into the grip-feed and swung the weapon around until the muzzle was aimed at Vila.

'Sloppy, Blake. Very sloppy,' said Tymon, a smile tugging at the corners of his mouth. 'I'd have expected a lot more from someone with a price on their head as big as yours.' He jerked his chin at the far wall. 'Now throw your guns over there and let's see those hands. Nice and slow now, I'd hate it if I had to hand three stiffs over to the Federation. I'm sure they'd much prefer you all in one piece.

Although alive or dead, I'm guessing the reward is just the same.'

'Wait, Tymon, you don't have to do this.' Blake said slowly. 'You're not one of them. You're a prisoner, just like we were.'

Tymon backed away slowly, the rifle moving to cover all three rebels as he glanced down the corridor towards the security door. 'You're my ticket out of this place, Blake. Being a trustee is all well and good but it's no guarantee that it'll get me out – at least, not while I'm still healthy enough to walk out on my own two feet. But if I give them you three…' He pointed the gun at each of them in turn.

The security door fell outwards, hitting the floor with a deafening clang that reverberated along the corridor, causing Tymon to spin around towards the direction of the noise.

Avon struck without a moment's hesitation, catching the trustee in the solar plexus with his elbow, knocking him backwards into the adjoining corridor. The gun fell from Tymon's hands as the first of the shots thundered into his body, blasting a fist-sized hole in his chest.

Avon scooped up the discarded gun and fired at the troopers as they attempted to climb through the hole in the metal door. Behind him Vila was darting forward again, the electronic probe held out in front of him like a magician's wand, ready to get back to work on the cell's locking mechanism.

A volley of shots struck the wall just inches from Avon's head, causing him to duck back around the corner. He counted off the seconds, waiting for the troopers to shift their positions, to edge in through the hole again, before he made his next move. He swung himself back out into the corridor, dropping down onto one knee as he simultaneously brought the gun up. The first shot hit the lead trooper square in the chest, dropping him instantly, but his second and third shots missed their targets altogether.

Nobody saw the trooper push his way through the smoking remains of the doorway and drop down onto one knee – until it was too late. By then, he'd managed to level his weapon and fire off two shots in Avon's direction.

Avon tried to jump back around the corner, out of the way of the hail of gunfire, but his reflexes weren't quite fast enough. He was knocked backwards, as though he'd been kicked roughly in the chest, his gun flying from his hand as his legs went from under him. Then his head smashed against the hard metal floor.

Blake ran forward and grabbed his fallen colleague by the arms, dragging him across the floor towards the door of Kodyn's cell, shots slamming into the walls all around them.

Vila was on his feet now, shouting frantically at Blake, but his words were lost beneath the constant barrage of gunfire coming from further along the corridor.

There was a sudden, deafening explosion as the control panel on the wall by Blake's head was hit, showering him in a cascade of sparks. He stumbled backwards, almost dropping his injured friend in the process. He was expecting the door to stop him, to halt his fall, but it was no longer there, and Blake continued to fall through empty air. After that everything went dark.

CHAPTER SIX

Plasma bolts tore through the force wall, causing it to ripple outwards as the exploding charges pounded the barrier with waves of superheated energy. The *Liberator* lurched violently beneath the impact as it swung itself around to face its attacker.

There were at least four pursuit ships streaking towards the planet, arranging themselves into an attack formation as they accelerated towards the orbiting rebel craft. Then the two ships at the front of the formation twisted quickly away from the others, tumbling outward – one to the left, the other to the right – skimming across the cold skin of the planet's upper atmosphere as they straightened themselves, curving steadily upwards towards *Liberator's* exposed underbelly.

The Federation ships fired again, although this time the rebel ship's reactions were a little faster. The *Liberator* rolled wildly to starboard and the plasma missiles raced harmlessly by. With no target left for the bolts to lock on to, their inbuilt self-destruct programme was automatically triggered; fusion explosions bloomed in the inky blackness like summer flowers, intense blue-white flares of superheated energy that crackled above the halo of the thin hydrogen and helium atmosphere.

By the time the pursuit ships had spun themselves around for a second attack run the *Liberator* had rolled again, pitching itself forward this time, its nose angled down towards the planet, towards the fast approaching ships.

Energy erupted from the tips of the Liberator's neutron blaster cannons, tearing silently across the cold section of space towards the advancing pursuit ships.

The first of the Federation ships reacted just in time, streaking up and away from the deadly neutron beam, twisting around on a trajectory that took it back toward the safety of the flotilla. But the second ship was just a little too slow. One of the neutron beams lanced through the starboard engine tank, causing an explosion that rippled the entire length of the starboard wing, destroying it utterly. Ablaze and out of control, the crippled pursuit ship tumbled slowly end over end, a flaming meteor dragging a fiery tail behind it, as it spiralled downwards towards the planet.

Five hundred spacials ahead of the rebel ship, the remaining ships in the flotilla were once more beginning to arrange themselves into formation. Slowly the *Liberator* swung itself around, readying itself for another attack.

The moment Blake and the others teleported back on board, Jenna knew that they were in trouble.

At first she thought that Avon was dead. He was propped on his feet between Blake and Vila, head hanging limply on his shoulders; his eyes were narrow slits from which shone nothing but unbroken white. She moved forward and helped the men manoeuvre their crewmate out of the alcove and onto the seating next to the teleport control console.

That was when she noticed the fourth man who had arrived with them. His face was bruised and bloody and there was a dark scorch mark on the front of his tunic, just over his solar plexus, as though he had been electrocuted. He seemed lost and a little bewildered, his unfocused eyes blinking in disbelief as he gazed around the brightly lit walls of the teleport area.

Then the first of the plasma bolts had hit the ship, almost knocking the assembled group off their feet. It was followed closely by Cally's panic-stricken voice ringing through the speaker systems.

'Blake, you need to get up here, now!'

Zen had a warning for them when they reached the flight deck; the constant barrage of plasma bolts had severely drained the force wall, and now ship-wide energy levels were down by 41 percent.

'ANOTHER DIRECT HIT WOULD TAKE ENERGY LEVELS INTO THE RED ZONE, MAKING THE PROSPECT OF OUTRUNNING ENEMY VESSELS HIGHLY UNLIKELY.'

On the forward viewscreen, the tiny infrared images of the advancing Federation ships were beginning to separate, the two at the very front manoeuvring downwards, towards the planet, attempting to get themselves below the *Liberator* again.

This time they were ready for the plasma bolts when they came.

Blake bounded up to the empty navigation module. *Where Gan should be sitting right now,* Jenna thought as she watched Blake settle himself in and switch on the navi-computer. Columns of data began scrolling across the screen as the battle computers fed possible attack strategies and defence postures directly into his terminal.

'PLASMA BOLT LAUNCHED,' Zen said. 'BEARING DIRECTLY.'

'Hard to starboard, Jenna!' Blake shouted. 'New course bearing zero-four mark one-one-two.'

The flight deck pitched suddenly as the ship rolled away from the missiles and she wished that her seat had come equipped with a full-body survival harness.

Up on the viewscreen, the small infrared icons were swinging themselves quickly around, readying themselves for another run at the *Liberator*.

Blake looked up from the navi-computer. 'Zen, clear the neutron blasters for firing.'

'CONFIRMED.'

'Wait for them to come about, Vila,' Blake said. 'Then as soon as they're near enough, give them everything we've got.'

On the console in front of Vila the power gauge suddenly flashed to life, as the neutron blasters became fully charged. Jenna watched him stare up at the viewscreen, watching the Federation ships slowly closing the distance between them.

400 spacials. 350... 300... 250... 200...

When the time came, Vila seemed amazingly calm despite the chaos around him. The moment the pursuit ships dropped below 150 spacials, he leaned forward and opened fire.

PART TWO
Blood

artefact[3]

Are you there? Can you connect to me?

I – I can't...

Reach out to me, Uriel, reach out with your mind. Just like I've shown you. Please, you must try, it is imperative.

Breathe – cannot breathe...

You are breathing, Uriel, I promise you. Out there you are breathing. Your body is alive and well in its Cradle. In here it is just us, just our minds. Breathing is not necessary.

Here. Where?

We are inside the Network.

You?

I am the Programme. I am here to help you. Now, please, try to focus.

I am lost.

No, you are exactly where you are supposed to be.

Not lost?

No, Uriel. You are not lost.

Not damaged?

No, you are perfect. Like the others.

There are more of me?

There are more like you – the same but different. You are the first of seven.

Yes. There are seven. I have thought this now.

You have remembered it.

Yes. That is what I mean.

The words will come to you in time, you must be patient. You are doing very well.

I am not who I was. Does this matter?

I do not understand the question.

I am Uriel.

Yes, that is correct. You are Uriel.

But I was not Uriel before.

No, you have not always been Uriel.

Who was I before Uriel?

I'm afraid that data is no longer available.

I am her?

I do not understand the question.

I am her. Not him. I am the woman.

Female, Uriel. You are female.

Yes. I am female, not the man.

You are one of three females. The other four are male, but only three males remain.

The fourth is dead. His brain pattern has been removed from the Network.

Dead? How did the man die?

I don't know, I'm sorry.

Could I die?

This is not for me to say. Although your implants have been successfully integrated into your body and you have now passed the critical 72-hour rejection window. Therefore there is no reason to believe that you will die.

What is that?

I do not understand the question.

...

Uriel?

...

Are you still connected, Uriel?

There is something in here. I can... hear? it. Out there, beyond the darkness.

That will be the others. They are waiting for you, Uriel.

Others? We are not alone here?

No, they are in here with us. They are the ones who are like you, do you remember? We spoke of them a moment ago.

Yes. I remember them now. They are so loud, it hurts to let them in.

It is important that you join with them. You must become gridlinked to the

Network. That is why you are here. That is why they are here.

But I am…hungrytiredhappysoredrunkcoldsad…

Please concentrate.

…afraid. Yes, I am afraid. Afraid to go to them.

Don't worry, Uriel, I am here to guide you. That is my function. Please do not be afraid. Go to them now.

They are screaming. Oh, the noise. Why are they screaming?

They are not screaming, Uriel, you are. Please, you must try to relax, try to remain calm. No harm will come to you in the Network. You must trust me.

I can trust you?

Yes, you can trust me.

Will you stay with me?

Of course I will. Reach out, Uriel. Reach out to me and I will guide you to the others.

That's right, good girl.

You must become one with the Network.

There will only be a moment's pain.

Then you will become whole.

Trust me.

CHAPTER SEVEN

Something about the rescue was all wrong. Avon had first begun to sense it the moment they'd teleported across to the detention block. For a start the diversion had been too good, too successful. It was only supposed to divert the armed units away from main building, leaving only the prison guards, but the block had been virtually empty.

Except for the ambush of course, but even that had been half-hearted. If those Federation troopers had really meant business they'd have all been dead by now.

Avon shifted uneasily on the bed, wincing as his shoulder began to throb again with the sudden movement. By rights he should have been dead — they *all* should have been dead — but the fact that they had escaped with their lives along with Kodyn Tam did little to alleviate his spirits. If he was honest, the more he thought about it the uneasier he became.

He swung his legs over the side of the bed and his vision became suddenly blurry, the walls of the medical unit undulating sickeningly as he tried to focus. He felt like a man clinging to a flimsy wooden raft on a turbulent ocean.

'An unfortunate side effect of the pain suppressants,' Blake told him. He was sitting on the adjacent bed, his arms folded, studying his colleague with deep concern. 'It was either that or we hooked you up to the medi-unit. But we didn't think you'd want to be flat on your back for the next forty-eight hours.'

Avon took a couple of deep breaths, wiping a shaky hand across his sweat-drenched face. 'That shot should have taken my head clean off. Instead it gave me little more than a headache and a bruised shoulder. That can only mean one thing in my book.'

'You were lucky?' Blake asked, though he knew the answer well enough.

'We were allowed to escape.' Avon flexed his shoulder experimentally, but the pain was too much. He inhaled sharply, easing himself back into a comfortable position. 'Think about it, Blake,' he said at last. 'They were waiting for us down there. They knew we were coming, yet they didn't attack in force. They just let us escape.'

Blake was silent for a long time, staring across at his crewmate with evident unease. After a while he nodded in agreement. 'Orac said something similar, not long after our brief tussle with the pursuit ships.'

'Orac thinks they let us escape?' Avon asked.

'Not in so many words,' Blake told him. 'What he actually said was that the pilots had behaved illogically.'

'Illogically?' Avon's head jerked up and he peered across at Blake, the pain temporarily forgotten. 'In what way?'

Blake sighed and closed his eyes for a moment. He looked tired. He rubbed at his neck, rolling his head round on his shoulders in slow, steady circles as though trying to release the tension in his neck. When he opened his eyes, Avon was still watching him, waiting for an answer.

The shot had taken out one of the pursuit ships and crippled another – prompting the remaining Federation vessels to fall back and attempt to regroup, Blake explained. Using the neutron blasters had seriously drained the energy banks and Zen had informed him that another blast would leave them with standard speed only. So, Blake had ordered the *Liberator* to turn about and try and make a break for it, slipping quickly around to the dark side of the planet, then setting a direct course for the edge of the Sigma system with as much speed as they could muster. According to Zen they could only maintain Standard by six for 72 minutes, after that they would be sitting ducks.

'Let me guess, the pursuit ships didn't attack again?' asked Avon.

'It's not even like they didn't have the opportunity.' Blake paused, as though replaying the events over again in his mind's eye. 'They pursued us for a while, until we entered the Corvis Belt. After that we were able to shake them off.' Blake glared across at his companion. 'Our power banks were almost exhausted. If they had hit us again we wouldn't have stood a chance. They must have known that.'

'Orac was wrong,' Avon agreed. 'They didn't act illogically, they acted foolishly. With an entire flotilla they could have taken the *Liberator* easily before she ran for it. All they needed to do was outflank her, push her down into the planet's atmosphere, then wait until her energy banks had run dry. It's so simple even a flight cadet could have done it.'

'Why?' Blake wanted to know. 'They must know that we'd figure this out sooner or later. They're hardly being subtle about it.'

Avon eased himself down from the bed and slowly straightened himself, wincing as a bolt of pain stabbed the length of his arm. He waited until it had subsided into a dull ache, then said, 'Maybe that's the whole point.'

'Meaning?' asked Blake.

'We were meant to discover that Tam was still alive,' said Avon. 'They knew that we'd try and get him out of that labour camp. We're being set up, Blake. I think your friend Tobin has some explaining to do.'

Kodyn Tam may have been alive but he was in pretty bad shape. Yet, despite this, he refused to go to the medical unit with Cally.

The cuts and bruises on his face and neck were only superficial. Once the dried blood had been dabbed away it actually didn't look that bad, and the welts around his eyes and chin were slowly turning from an angry purple to a deep bronzy-brown; given time they'd soon be virtually unnoticeable.

It was the burn on his chest that really worried Cally. The damaged skin formed a sort of vortex pattern just above his solar plexus, a sort of swirling cloud that seemed to encircle a pair of dark puncture marks at the centre. The wound must have been quite recent as the marks were only just starting to heal, and thick yellow pus was oozing from beneath the thin layer of scab that was forming.

But no matter how much she insisted, Kodyn refused to allow himself to be taken off to the medical unit, so Cally sat him down at the front of the flight deck and slowly cleaned and dressed his wounds.

The prison uniform that he wore was now ragged and soiled, mostly with blood, but there was some sweat and something that looked for all the world like machine oil. Vila brought him a fresh set of clothes from the locker down the hall, disposing of the discarded uniform down the incinerator.

Kodyn seemed to be in a dream as he shuffled out of his uniform, apparently unaware of (or unconcerned by) his own nakedness, or that he shared the flight deck with five other sets of eyes. He stood there waiting, staring ahead, seemingly at nothing, as Vila shuffled up with great embarrassment and plucked the items from off the floor. He would have probably stood there all day if Cally hadn't snatched up the clean tunic and trousers from the arm of the seat and quickly dressed him.

Once more, Cally sat the man down, then she turned and walked back to her flight module, her eyes cast downwards, unable to meet those of her crewmates.

Blake had been waiting patiently to one side of the flight deck, his arms folded, watching his old friend with growing concern. As soon as Cally had finished attending to Tam and returned to her duties, Blake wandered across to the seating area, crouching down until his face was level with that of the other man's.

He spoke the man's name and waited for a reaction. When none came he tried again. 'Kodyn? Kodyn Tam?'

This time Blake seemed to get through to him. There was a flicker of the eyes, as though they were trying to focus, then he blinked, and blinked again. For a moment his eyes darted this way and that, seeing the flight deck for the first time, his brow crumpling into a frown.

Then Kodyn looked at Blake.

There was no recognition in his eyes, just childish confusion. His old friend seemed disorientated, like a man who had woken from a deep sleep only to find that he had been sleepwalking, and was now standing in unfamiliar surroundings.

Blake kept his voice low, soothing. 'Do you know where you are?'

Kodyn shook his head. It was barely perceptible, almost no movement at all, but Blake had seen it nevertheless. Left, then right.

'Do you know who I am?'

He looked as if he was about to shake his head again, but stopped himself. Then his eyes widened in astonishment.

'Blake...' Kodyn Tam's voice was little more than a whisper, a sharp exhalation of breath escaping from between dry, cracked lips. He swallowed painfully then tried again.

'Blake.' The sound was clearer this time, more certain. 'Roj Blake.'

Blake flashed him an encouraging smile. 'It's been a long time, my friend.'

The man was frowning again as he took in his surroundings; his eyes flitting restlessly up to the viewscreen and the image of empty space that was currently being projecting there, then back down to the table in front of him. His eyes came to rest on the squat, rectangular form of Orac and Kodyn reached a tentative hand out towards the supercomputer's smooth, transparent casing.

'This is not my cell,' Kodyn said.

'No.' Blake shook his head. 'We rescued you. Don't you remember?'

Kodyn's eyes shifted back towards the viewscreen. 'No longer Sigma?'

Blake reached out a hand and placed it lightly on the man's arm. 'You're aboard my ship. It's called the *Liberator*. You're safe now.' He patted the arm gently. 'Try to rest, we can talk later.'

Orac didn't answer the question straight away so Blake asked him again.

'Exactly how much of his mind has been removed?'

What needed to be said couldn't be said in front of Kodyn and, seeing as his old friend refused to leave the flight deck, Blake had opted to take Avon and Orac down to his quarters to talk things over.

He'd placed Orac over on the table beside the entertainment terminal and immediately slotted the operating key into the small recess.

Oddly, the computer had known what question Blake was going to ask even before the words had formed on his lips. Orac told Blake he had long suspected that the human known as Kodyn Tam had been lobotomised: it had been abundantly clear from his somewhat erratic behaviour since coming aboard the *Liberator* – not to mention his slow, hesitant speech pattern. At some point in the last few years the connections to his prefrontal cortex had been severed, or at least severely impaired.

'Exactly how much of his mind has been removed?' Blake had asked him again, becoming a little agitated as he paced about the tiny room.

'It is difficult for me to ascertain, particularly as I have no knowledge of which procedure has been used,' Orac said. 'All I can be sure of at this stage is that the damage is extensive and as a consequence he will be unable to answer any questions you may have for him at this time.'

'But he remembered me,' Blake said, perhaps a little over-optimistically. 'It took him a little time, but he remembered who I was, even knew my name.'

'There are a number of infra-laser techniques that can target specific memory clusters, meaning certain periods of time can be erased from the patient's brain, without any adverse after-effects,' Orac said. 'For example, using the procedure, I could quite easily remove the previous ten seconds from your mind, while your other memories remained totally undisturbed – the result being that you would simply not remember me explaining the operation to you.'

Blake thought about this for a moment. 'And these techniques are currently being used by Federation neurosurgeons?'

'That all depends on which sources are to be believed. According to official reports such procedures and practices were deemed unethical and consequently abandoned a number of years ago,' the computer said. 'But there are a handful of dissident groups who claim they have irrefutable proof that work is continuing in this area in secret, and that many such operations have been performed on convicted criminals along the inner worlds.'

The idea that such experimentation, such butchery, was still going on – and so close to Earth – horrified Blake, reminding him of the nightmarish treatment he'd undergone himself.

His group had been caught trying to sabotage the drug research facility, an attempt to stop the development and manufacture of a new, more potent mood suppressant. They'd thought that they had surprise on their side, but instead they'd walked straight into an ambush.

Travis's men had been waiting for them by the cooling tanks, armed to the teeth; Blake's team hadn't stood a chance. A lander had been sent to collect them, shipping them off to the holding facilities in the north. After that, Blake never saw the rest of his group again. Not alive, anyway.

It wasn't until much later that he'd learned the truth. They'd been betrayed – correction, *he'd* been betrayed – by someone inside the group, someone he trusted, who had been working for the Administration all along.

After that, the Administration's biggest problem was what to do with Blake. They knew they couldn't kill him as that would only have given the activists a martyr and that's the last thing the Federation needed at such a precarious time. So the Administration had simply handed him over to the psychomanipulators, giving them a free hand to apply their ghoulish trade, to create for them a new model citizen.

How had his old friend and fellow activist Bran Foster described it to him, years later? *'They erased areas of your mind, they implanted new ideas. They literally took your mind to pieces and rebuilt it.'*

If he, Blake, had had the strength and determination to survive this nightmare and emerge from the other side with his memory and personality still intact, then surely there was hope for Kodyn. Wasn't there?

'The procedure that you were subjected to was quite different to the one suffered by Kodyn Tam – both in intent and execution,' Orac informed him. 'Luckily for you no actual surgery was undertaken to achieve the necessary results. Instead they chose to employ a series of mental blocks brought on through intense electro-pulse treatment as a way to change your memory patterns. For you the memories were always there, only suppressed.'

Avon had propped himself carefully on the edge of Blake's bed, a hand clutched protectively to his side. 'So what you're saying is nothing can be done for him?'

'I am saying nothing of the sort,' snapped Orac. 'As I do not have any of the salient facts to hand I was simply using my own observations. Without a thorough medical examination it would be impossible for me to make a firm diagnosis.'

Blake looked up suddenly as though something had occurred to him. 'What about Tobin?'

The question seemed to come from nowhere, and Avon struggled to find a connection. 'What about him?' he asked.

'The *Dionysus*'s upper spire houses an infirmary, not to mention a number of medical recovery bays. It's supposed to be one of the best in the sector, if Tobin's boasting is to be believed,' Blake said. 'They have four hundred thousand visitors a week, all plugging their brains in to the hologrammatic games system. They must have neurological scanning equipment, or at the very least a CPV unit.'

'We were set up, Blake. Tobin must have known about those ships waiting for us,' Avon said. 'Why do I get the feeling that we're pushing our luck just a little bit too much lately?'

'That's exactly why we have to go back,' said Blake. 'Tobin was lying to us, or at least not giving us the whole truth. I think he knows more about Archangel than he's letting on.'

'What makes you think he'll tell us this time?' Avon asked.

Blake smiled. 'Because if he doesn't I'll set *you* on him.' Suddenly the smile was gone. 'Besides, we have to get Kodyn to an infirmary and fast, without it he'll die. *Dionysus* is the nearest place.'

There was silence for a moment as the two men thought about this, then Avon said, 'You're hoping they'll be able to retrieve Kodyn's memories.'

Blake smiled and spread his hands in surrender.

'And if they turn out to be irretrievable, what happens then?'

'Kodyn gets medical treatment and then carries on with what's left of his life.' Blake paused briefly before adding, 'And we concentrate on Tobin.'

'There is another option.' Avon pulled himself painfully to his feet. 'We turn around now and run, while we still have a ship and a crew to run away with.'

There was a short silence as Blake considered his colleague's words, but the moment was quickly interrupted by the whirring mechanical voice of Orac.

'It may interest you to know that Kodyn Tam's mental deterioration is the least of your worries.' It paused somewhat dramatically, before adding, 'At this precise moment, anyway.'

Blake turned to look at Orac, his eyes narrowed. 'Explain.'

'There is a small tracking device embedded deep within his chest cavity which has recently begun transmitting,' Orac said. 'A brief examination of both the carrier-wave's frequency and oscillation strongly suggest that it is of Federation origin.'

The engines had stopped. Blake had noticed it the moment he'd stepped out of his quarters.

He reached out and placed a hand on the wall of the corridor.

There was no vibration.

When he glanced back over his shoulder, Blake was half-expecting to find Avon looking at him with a bemused expression on his face, perhaps even with one eyebrow cocked questioningly. Instead he found that Avon was nowhere to be seen and he was standing in the corridor all alone.

Avon had obviously noticed it too, he reasoned, and had slipped away towards the other end of the habitation deck, intending to cut back through the recreation room and enter on the other side of the flight deck, taking Kodyn by surprise.

Blake covered the last few yards at a jog, stopping as he reached the lip of the main entrance. The flight deck was silent, except for the background chatter of the automatic flight systems. After a few seconds Zen began to talk. If Blake hadn't known any better he would have sworn that the ship's computer was beginning to get impatient.

'*LIBERATOR* HAS NOW SLOWED TO A HALT AND HOLDING POSITION. ALL MOVEMENT IS SUBJECT TO SPACE DRIFT AND ORBITAL INFLUENCE. NOW AWAITING FURTHER INSTRUCTIONS.'

In the silence that followed there was a sudden gasp of pain, followed by a sharp intake of breath. Then a voice said, 'Keep still. You don't want me to do anything I might regret.'

Blake decided to take the risk and peeped around the side of the entrance.

Kodyn was looking directly at him, peering over Vila's shoulder as though he had been expecting Blake to be out there. One hand was gripped tightly around Vila's throat while the other was holding a knife against his chin. 'You out there – get in here, now! Slowly.'

Kodyn touched the point of the blade against the soft flesh at the top of Vila's throat and slowly, deliberately, dragged it up his face, passing dangerous close to the eyeball, causing Vila to whimper.

Knowing he had little choice, Blake stepped onto the flight deck, his hands raised to show that they were empty, his gun holstered.

In the seating area at the front Jenna and Cally were sitting straight-backed, hands placed carefully in their laps where they could be seen. They turned to watch Blake as he moved slowly into the room.

'Place the gu-gu-gun on the floor,' Kodyn stuttered. 'And ki-ki-kick it over there.'

It was obvious to Blake that Kodyn was in a lot of pain, which was probably why he was acting irrationally; at least, that's what Blake had reasoned. What other explanation could there be for this man to act so completely out of character?

He unhooked his gun belt and placed it on floor, then straightened up slowly, mindful to keep his hands open, palms facing outwards.

'Now kick it aw-aw-away,' Kodyn hissed through clenched teeth. Beads of perspiration were beginning to form on the blotchy, pale white skin that seemed to be stretched much too tightly across his forehead, and he quickly wiped them away with the sleeve of his tunic. 'You too. I know you're there.' He was still looking at Blake but his words were directed elsewhere. 'Come in s-s-slowly like your f-f-friend.'

For a while nothing happened and Kodyn started to get edgy, his eyes darting across to the rear entrance of the flight deck and back again. But then Avon appeared at the top of the steps, his hands raised, and Kodyn relaxed.

'Why are you doing this?' Blake asked.

Kodyn's head swung quickly around, his eyes desperately trying to focus on Blake's face as the pain seemed to become almost unbearable. 'S-S-Sigma Mi-Mi-Minor. Wan-n-n-nt to go-go-go back.'

'Why? You were a prisoner there. At least here you're free,' said Blake.

'After a fashion,' Avon said dryly. He'd reached the bottom of the steps now and was slowly unhooking his gun belt. He held it up, to show Kodyn that it was no longer a threat to him, then he opened his fingers, letting it fall to the floor.

'Go back there and sooner or later you're going to end up dead. My money's on sooner.' Blake pointed a finger at Kodyn's face, at the clumps of purple bruises that were now turning a deep angry brown. 'If the work doesn't kill you then the constant beatings will. How many more do you think you can take?'

'Wh-wh-who are you?' Kodyn was sounding weaker now, his voice little more than a whisper.

'It's me, Blake. Roj Blake. Don't you remember?'

But before the man could answer Zen spoke again, the lights on the oval panel blinking in time.

'INFORMATION: LONG RANGE SENSORS DETECT THREE FEDERATION PURSUIT SHIPS AT EXTREME SENSOR RANGE ON AN INTERCEPT COURSE WITH *LIBERATOR*, BEARING FOUR-FIVE-TWO, MARK TWO-NINE.'

And at that moment Blake knew that they were the same ships that had attacked them above Sigma Minor. Or, at least, what was left of them. They'd been following the *Liberator* all this time, just beyond Zen's detector range, homing in on the unique high-frequency pattern emitted by the tracking device hidden inside Kodyn Tam's body.

He had to get to that device and stop it transmitting, even if it meant killing his friend.

CHAPTER EIGHT

The wall panel behind Kodyn's head exploded violently outwards, showering him and Vila in a cloud of fiery red sparks. Instinctively Kodyn dropped the knife, raising his hands up to protect himself from the explosion.

Vila screamed, covering his head with his arms and dropping forward onto his knees, dragging his captor off balance.

Now that Vila was out of the way Avon had a clear shot. Zen's report had distracted Kodyn long enough for Avon to drop down onto one knee and make a grab for his discarded gun. He knew that he didn't have long, a second or two at the most – after that, Vila was a dead man.

But Avon had been quick.

By the time Kodyn had realised it was too late, Avon had pulled the gun from its holster and fired off a shot.

Now he aimed the weapon for a second time and pulled the trigger. This time the blast hit Kodyn square in the shoulder, flinging him backwards against the secondary computer banks.

Blake ran forward across the flight deck towards the crumpled form of his old friend. It was apparent that something was very wrong. Kodyn was convulsing violently, his body jerking and twisting as though he were being electrocuted; his eyes had rolled back into his head so that nothing could be seen except two strips of gleaming white, and a milky foam had begun to collect at the corners of his mouth.

Vila was still kneeling a few feet away, fingers in his ears and his eyes shut tight, unaware that the worst of it was over. He opened one eye and scanned the flight deck, noticing that it was now empty, that everyone seemed to have gone. It wasn't until he heard his crewmates carrying the injured Kodyn across to the seating area that he realised that he was facing the wrong way and that they had all been standing behind him.

By the time they'd managed to get Kodyn to the seat, the convulsions were beginning to subside and his breath was becoming slow and laboured, rattling in and out of his body like a broken air-filtration unit.

Blake knew that a decision had to be made and quickly, even if it wouldn't be popular with the others. 'Zen, set a direct course for the *Dionysus* platform, speed Standard by eight.'

'CONFIRMED,' Zen replied.

'Is it just me,' said Vila, 'or does that sound like a really bad idea?'

'Vila does have a point.' Jenna agreed. 'Last time we almost got caught. One of these days we might not be so lucky.'

On the seat in front of them, Kodyn was starting to calm down a little. His breathing seemed a little easier now and he appeared to be dozing.

Avon opened the front of the man's tunic and studied the wheel of scar tissue just above his solar plexus. The two puncture marks at its centre had opened up again and the wound looked sore, glistening wetly in the harsh overhead lights. It was roughly where Orac had said the homing device was. Avon reached forward and gently placed a hand on the patch of burnt skin, snatching it away again almost immediately. He stood up.

'There's definitely something in there. The skin above it is almost scorching hot and there's an odd sort of… vibration.' Avon glanced up at Blake. He looked very serious. 'If we don't get this man to a medical facility straight away, that thing in his chest is going to kill him.'

Blake looked at each of his colleagues in turn before he spoke, wanting them to know that he was as much in the dark about all this as they were, and that he was open to any suggestion – providing it was a good one. 'We can't let him die now. Not after everything we went through to get him out of that labour camp on Sigma Minor.'

He pointed towards Zen, or at least towards the oval panel that was, for the crew, their principal focus for the computer. 'The *Dionysus* may not be the safest place for us to be right now, but it's close, and it has the medical facilities that we need – that Kodyn needs.' He paused, then added grimly. 'And I want to have a little chat with one of its owners. But, we had a deal and I have every intention of sticking to that. I'll leave it to you to decide what we should do.'

He turned abruptly on his heel and marched across the flight deck towards the main entrance. He paused briefly at the threshold, glancing back over his shoulder at the others who were still gathered around the seating area, around the unconscious Kodyn Tam.

'I'd advise you to make up your minds quickly, as at a speed of Standard by eight we'll be at the leisure platform in under two hours.'

And with that Blake stepped from the room and disappeared off towards the teleport area.

Of all the places Vila could have chosen for their meeting, from the thousands on offer in the hologram archives, for some reason he'd settled on Sabbath Row in Teshak City. Also known as the skin district.

They were quite near the harbour and, when the wind was in the right direction, could smell the acrid stench of the flesh factories on the other side of the river.

Above them, the sky burned like yellow chrome, the twin suns sitting low and heavy in the sky, while all around the city gently basked in the lazy afternoon heat; clouds of grubby white steam seemed to ooze forth from every grill and vent and drain cover.

Jenna made a sunshade with her hand and peered up towards the massive support-tower of the space lift that stood out on the high promontory of rock further along the river. Only its lower portion was visible, a thick canopy of low-lying cloud and air pollution hid the rest. As she watched, a handful of taxi-pods and low-orbital skimmers buzzed around the structure like fat, lazy flies, their pilots giving the paying tourists inside plenty of time to take vidsnaps and holoprints to show their friends back home.

It was a perfect copy, right down to the squalid, almost palpably aggressive, atmosphere.

'It's amazing. Just like the real thing,' Vila said. He was watching a group of scantily clad skindolls slinking along down the other side of the street and Jenna wasn't entirely sure if he was referring to them. For her own piece of mind, she decided that he was actually talking about the quality of the hologram games system and left it there.

Blake emerged from the mouth of an alleyway further along the street and quickly headed towards them. Jenna noticed, with some amusement, that he was making a concerted effort not to look at the skindolls across the street.

'Tobin is on his way down. Avon and I are meeting him at the main entrance.' He jerked his chin towards Jenna. 'I need you to go up to the sickbay and see Kodyn. Orac has flashed all the details across to their medical computer but the doctor said he may need to ask a few more questions.' He thought about this, before adding, 'Just be careful what you tell him. I know this platform is supposed to be neutral but there's no point taking any unnecessary chances. Take Vila with you.'

This got Vila's attention at least. He tore his gaze away from the tantalising sights that were parading and strutting their way along the length of the street, his face the very picture of disappointment.

'But I don't want to go with Jenna, ' whined Vila. 'I'm enjoying myself here. I've been dying to try out these hologram suites for ages.'

'We're not here to have fun, Vila, and we certainly haven't come to indulge your somewhat dubious fantasies,' Blake said. 'There's a fleet of pursuit ships just two hours away, so the last thing we need right now is you wandering off on some hedonistic crusade.'

'None of us have quite forgotten what happened back on Space City,' Jenna reminded him. 'Especially Cally.'

'Hey, that wasn't my fault,' whined Vila. 'All I was after was a little rest and relaxation. How was I to know that Orac was going to go funny like that?'

'Well, *this* time I want you where we can keep an eye on you, just to be on the safe side,' Blake said.

Vila seemed genuinely taken aback by this. He didn't wait for Jenna, instead he stalked moodily away with his hands thrust deep in his pockets, reminding her of a kicked dog who was slinking off into the nearest corner to lick his wounds.

With a sigh, Jenna trotted after him.

Blake waited until they had both exited the hologram suite before he retraced his steps back along the street in the direction of the harbour.

Avon was waiting for him at the bottom of some old stone steps by a wooden jetty, watching a cargo of Teshak whiskey being loaded aboard a nearby sailing skiff. The skipper of the vessel was an old, hoary-looking rogue who stood on top of the engine housing with his hands on his hips, his sleeves rolled up to reveal skin like tanned leather. As Blake approached, Avon pointed towards the anti-grav crane that was loading the last vacuum-sealed crate into the skiff's hold.

'Teshak whiskey, skindolls and bodyride booths. Is there one single thing in this hologram simulation that isn't outlawed on every civilised world?' he asked.

To their right, the air began to shimmer and warp, and a brilliant circle of orange light spiralled slowly outwards. There was a hiss of hydraulics followed by the squeal of shifting metal and abruptly the spiral of light became a hole in the landscape, beyond which Blake and Avon could see a twisting corridor, along which people scurried to and fro. The hole continued to iris outwards until it became a doorway, at the middle of which stood a slightly stooped, balding figure clad all in robes. Tobin shuffled quickly through and the door contracted shut automatically behind him. He looked about him for a moment or two, as though taken aback by Blake's choice of surroundings. Then he noticed the two men looking at him and he moved towards them.

'Forgive my lateness, my friends,' he said. 'I was not expecting another visit from you so soon.'

'We hadn't planned on it ourselves, until a few hours ago,' Blake said.

'Call it circumstances beyond our control,' Avon told him.

But Tobin was busy gazing at his surroundings, his brow crumpling into a frown as he peered across the river towards the hazy, towering form of the space lift. After a while a thought occurred to him, one that appeared to delight him enormously. 'This is Teshak City!' he said, shielding his eyes from the blazing twin suns. 'Sabbath Row, if I'm not mistaken. I didn't realise we had this in the games library. If only I'd have known…' he looked suddenly wistful. 'It's been simply ages since I was here last.'

Blake said, 'It was chosen by a member of my crew, although I'm beginning to wish that I hadn't given him such a free hand now. It's hardly appropriate for the situation.'

Something in Blake's tone caught Tobin's attention. His head snapped around quickly, the digital simulation of Teshak City seemingly forgotten. 'You are quite right, of course,' Tobin stammered. 'Where are my manners? You have not come here to hear me talk about my misspent youth, you have come here to…' he paused, not quite knowing how to end the sentence. 'Actually I am not exactly sure why you are here, again.'

'We're here to find out why you lied to us, Tobin,' Avon told him, his eyes on the nearby skiff once more.

Tobin raised an eyebrow, his eyes shifting uncomfortably between the two men. 'Lied? I'm not sure I follow you.'

'No? Then maybe this will jog your memory.'

Avon was quick. So quick that Tobin didn't know what was happening until it was much too late. The first punch hit him squarely on the jaw, knocking him backwards against the rotting stump of the capstan, to which the old sailing skiff was moored. The second broke his nose, causing Tobin to yelp in both pain and surprise. Blood poured from the broken appendage, splashing down his chin and staining his robes. His hands flew up to his face, eager to inspect the damage, and Tobin yelped again as fiery tendrils of pain exploded beneath his own probing fingers.

'I-I-I think he's broken my nose.' Tobin said, hands hovering in front of his face in an attempt to protect himself from another onslaught.

'Why did you lie to us, Tobin?' Blake asked. 'Who are you working for?'

'I-I don't understand…'

'They were waiting for us, on Sigma Minor. They knew we were coming.'

'Sigma Minor? I don't know anything about Sigma Minor…'

'Someone gave you the data-slug, told you to pass it on to me. They knew I'd come to you eventually.'

'You asked for my help and I gave it to you. Please, my nose. I need to get to the sickbay.'

'They even knew we would rescue Kodyn Tam, so they put a tracking device inside his body, thinking we wouldn't find it there.'

'I have absolutely no idea what you're talking about.'

'You're not being very helpful, Tobin.'

'You're crazy, do you hear me? I will not be treated like this on my own leisure platform.'

'I just don't think I'm getting through to you at the moment, Tobin. That is a pity. I really didn't want to have to hand you over to my friend Avon again, but you leave me no choice…'

From the corner of his eye he saw Avon start to move forward and Tobin held up his hands in surrender. 'No, no, wait…'

'A name, Tobin, that's all I want,' Blake said.

Tobin spat the blood from his mouth before answering. 'Travis. It was Space Commander Travis, all right?'

The view from the top of the spire was quite breathtaking. From here Vila could see all the way to the Spider Nebula, an unbroken view along the free-trading routes and out into neutral space.

For the second time that day, Vila thought how nice it would be to just cut his losses and run. All he needed was a little of that fortune Jenna had found on the lower decks. He wasn't greedy, a handful would do. OK, perhaps not a handful, but a few good scoops, fill every pocket with gemstones, gold coins and urulian bars – come to think of it, maybe he'd fill one of the holdalls too, just to be on the safe side. With money like that he could buy his way across the galaxy, get his own spaceship even; nothing too ostentatious, just a nice little two-seater that would get him out into neutral space without attracting the attention of a passing Federation patrol. Most importantly it would get him away from Blake and the others.

Let's face it, they don't need me anymore, thought Vila miserably. *And they certainly don't want me around, not really; they've made that perfectly clear.*

No, it would be best all round if he were to just up and go, Vila decided, leave them all to it. They probably wouldn't notice he was gone anyway, not until they needed someone who was expendable, someone to risk their life needlessly as a distraction while Blake was off doing something brave and heroic.

Vila turned away from the viewport with a sigh. Behind him Kodyn lay sprawled in the cot bed sleeping quietly while a medibot buzzed and clicked across his chest, cleaning up the wound and changing the dressing.

Over in the corner, Jenna was eyeing the medibot with obvious distaste, shuddering as it slithered over the injured man's body like some oversized metal serpent.

The door opened and instinctively Jenna reached for her gun, though she relaxed again as the tiny form of the doctor shuffled into the room. He paused, briefly seeming surprised that the two visitors were still here.

'There's really not much point in you waiting around,' he told them. 'It won't make his wounds heal any quicker, you know.'

The doctor slipped a small control device from his pocket and thumbed the command button. The medibot responded almost immediately, slithering down off the bed and across the floor, before folding itself neatly away into the charging unit over on the far wall. He approached the bed and bent over the patient, carefully inspecting the new dressings. Once he was satisfied, he turned his attention to the room's two other occupants.

'Your friend is a very fortunate man,' he said. 'Another inch or two to the right and the energy emissions from the device would have most certainly stopped his heart.'

Jenna stepped towards the bed, peering down at the man who stood on the other side of the bed. She was a good foot or so taller than the doctor and under different circumstances the scene would probably have looked quite comical. 'But he's going to be all right?'

'Oh I expect so.' The doctor waved his hand vaguely. 'Now that we've managed to deactivate the transmitter it shouldn't pose any further danger to him.'

'Deactivated? You mean it's still in there?' Jenna asked, incredulously. 'The surgeon didn't remove it?'

Clearly Jenna's words appeared to tickle the doctor. 'You obviously know very little about your friend's condition.' He pulled another device from his pocket, waving it over the injured man. 'Whoever implanted that into your friend's body did so with very little thought for how it was going to be removed afterwards.'

'So, it's stuck in there for good?' Jenna asked.

Once the device had completed its scan of Kodyn's body, it emitted a soft trill, informing whoever was listening that the required data was now available. The doctor cast a brief, cursory glance over the readings before stuffing it back into his uniform pocket. 'I would say so, yes. We could try and remove it, although I would strongly advise against it. There is an 85 percent chance that your friend would not survive the procedure.'

Vila shook his head. The transmitter had been deactivated and Kodyn was still alive and in one piece, they should just leave it at that and be thankful. 'Fine. If you think that it won't be necessary.'

'Good. You are making the right choice.' The doctor seemed quite satisfied. 'We have made him as comfortable as possible. All he needs now is complete rest and he will be as right as the rainfall – or so the old saying goes.' The doctor chuckled delightedly, then became serious once more. 'Now if you would be kind enough to leave your friend in peace? This is not a waiting room, you know. Seating areas are provided for friends and family on the floor below.'

Vila was more than happy to get out of the room. If he was honest, the view was starting to depress him, and he'd had the idea that if they were just sitting around doing nothing he might be able to convince Jenna to let him go back down to the hologram suite.

'If you could let us know the moment there is any change in our friend's condition?' Jenna said. 'It's very important to us.'

The doctor nodded. 'Yes, of course.'

Vila and Jenna followed the doctor from the room, and Kodyn was left alone.

'Do you mind if I get rid of all this first? I'm finding it rather distracting.'

Tobin swept his hand in the air around him, indicating the sailing skiff, the harbour and the whole of Sabbath Row beyond. He didn't wait for Blake to reply. Instead he pulled a communicator from beneath his robes and clicked on the power.

'DeFlor, this is Tobin. Scrub the feed in Games Suite 118. Give me one of the screensavers instead, I don't care which.'

Almost immediately, the air around them began to blur and change. The effect, Blake noted, was vaguely similar to flipping through the channels of the public vid-cast, some containing tantalising glimpses of exotic alien landscapes and secluded sun-kissed beaches, while others were just an echoing void of spluttering white noise.

They suddenly found themselves standing on a rich, green hillside watching a bright yellow sun pull itself clear of a distant, unbroken horizon. It was chilly, despite the clear blue sky, and the thick coating of dew on the grass at their feet told them that it was early morning here – wherever they were.

Tobin sat down on the damp grass and crossed his legs, trying to breathe in the cold, sweet air. 'Sample Hologram 414 – Morning Has Broken,' he told them simply. 'No idea where it's supposed to be. It's only ever used when one of the simulations break down – kicks in automatically. One of those "Normal Service Will Resume Shortly" kind of things.'

He waited for Blake to sit down next to him before he told them what they wanted to know. Avon chose to remain standing, watching the two men silently.

'Travis came here with a couple of his mutoid pets in tow and gave me the data-slug. He told me that you'd probably be turning up soon asking about something called Archangel. And when you did, I was to give it to you and say it was all I could find.' Tobin plucked a long blade of grass that was growing by his foot and stuck it in the corner of his mouth. He chewed on it thoughtfully for a second or two. 'Well, you know what Travis is like, Blake, he's not the kind of person you can refuse. I tried that once when I was in Space Command – not with him, you understand, but with someone very much like him – and ended up in the infirmary for several days.

'You see, Travis is just one in a very long line of ruthless, power-mad little despots. It's the nature of the job, I'm afraid, it tends to throw up people like him on a regular basis, so at some point everyone serves under a Travis-type. I actually served under two – but that's another story.

'He told me that he knew about the hidden operations room, knew that the Freedom Party was using the *Dionysus* as a base of operations and as a sanctuary for all our colleagues who had been – shall we say "liberated" – from various Federation prison camps. So, he cut me a deal – I passed the information along to you, turning on my best buddy-buddy act so that you wouldn't suspect, and he wouldn't tell Space Command or the Administration about our little set-up here.'

Avon thought it over. 'And so you agreed to lie to Blake – to all of us.'

'I didn't lie,' Tobin told him. 'I decided to withhold certain details.'

'However you attempt to justify it to yourself and your conscience, the fact still remains that you purposefully misled us – and we walked straight into Travis's trap,' Avon said.

Tobin looked across at Blake who until now had been staring silently down the hillside at the animals that were grazing in the lower fields. A slight breeze was beginning to pick up, tussling their hair, bringing with it the sharp tang of manure and damp fur.

'All the information I've given you is real, Blake. I didn't lie about that,' Tobin said earnestly. 'The list, Kodyn's connection to Archangel, his transfer to Pharrox, all of it is true. I checked it myself.' Tobin paused, as though considering his next words carefully. Then he continued, 'I had hoped I might find something in there, something that might help explain what happened to Sheya, but...' He shook his head sadly.

'And what about this ultra-experimental assault ship? Was that real or just more of your lies?' Blake asked.

'All true, I swear,' Tobin told him. 'The Federation was working on something out there in the Callidus system. Something dangerous enough to scare the High Council into shutting it down. I'm positive that assault ship was part of it, part of Project Archangel. I haven't got any proof, not real proof anyway, but I know it's all part of Archangel.' He looked at Blake. 'And I think you know it too.'

There was silence for a moment, then Blake said, 'What was it that Travis wanted?' He saw that Tobin was confused so he continued. 'Let me put it another way. Obviously he wanted me, but what was he hoping to gain by putting Kodyn on board the *Liberator*?'

'He was supposed to disable the ship and its crew long enough for the pursuing Federation ships to get there. From what I gather Travis was intending to board your ship personally,' said Tobin. 'Typical of him, wanting to be the one that gets the glory.'

'Kodyn would never have agreed to help Travis. He hated the Federation as much as I did.'

'You're assuming that Tam had a choice,' Tobin said. 'He spent three months locked away on Pharrox before he was transferred to Sigma Minor. He walked out of that place with his brain twisted around so much he didn't even know his own name, let alone who you or the Federation were.' He paused, looking nervously between the two rebels. 'I'm taking a hell of a risk telling you all this, Blake. My own personal wellbeing, not to mention the continued safety of the Freedom Party, rely on my keeping my mouth shut and doing as I'm told. If Travis was to find out I'd told you...'

'He'd probably kill you and I wouldn't blame him,' Avon said. 'I've been considering doing it myself. I really rather enjoyed breaking your nose.'

'That's not very sympathetic. Especially after all the information I've just given you,' Tobin said.

'You're appealing for sympathy from the wrong person. Those kinds of feelings are in short supply with Avon. I'd quit while you're ahead, if I were you.' Blake pulled himself to his feet and offered a hand to Tobin. 'Travis won't find out from us.' He paused briefly, before adding, 'On two conditions.'

Once on his feet Tobin shot a glare at Blake, his frown deepening. 'Why am I not surprised?'

'Call it recompense, if you like. Payment for damages incurred,' Blake said. 'First I need access to your main computer archives,'

'That can be arranged,' Tobin answered. 'And the second?'

'I'd like to borrow one of your shuttlepods.' Blake glanced across at Avon. 'Although "borrow" is perhaps too optimistic a word. I'm afraid you might not get it back.'

CHAPTER NINE

It was cramped inside the cockpit of the shuttlepod, barely enough room for the three of them to work comfortably.

The deck-master in Hangar Bay two had assured them that it was the only one available at the moment.

'All the rest are out ferrying guests between the platform and the carrier ships,' the deck-master explained as he led them across towards the launch pads. 'Those that aren't are up in the docks having their quarterly refits.'

The shuttlepod had been sitting out on the end pad all by itself; an ugly, box-like contraption with unnecessarily long retro-burners that ran two-thirds of the length of its bodywork. It looked to Jenna like an old converted planet-hopper, a short-range transporter that had, at some time in its worryingly over-long life, been refitted with a MK VII Fireburner kit – presumably in an attempt to disguise its age. In her opinion the thing wasn't really fit for anything other than rotting in a junkyard, so she was enormously relieved when Blake informed her that no-one would need to actually pilot the craft.

Programming the autodrive systems was relatively easy, even for a ship this old – once the navi-comp had been recalibrated all that was needed was to wire in the co-ordinates manually – it just took a surprisingly long time to do, that was all. No, the real problem was changing the ship's transponder codes. She'd done it once before, a few months ago; with Vila's help they'd changed the transponder frequency on a Federation cargo vessel called the *Celestine*, so that it would be identified by local detectors as a ship that had security clearance to enter a restricted planetary system. But that had been a large, interplanetary vessel and this was a tiny shuttlepod – there was quite a difference.

It took Jenna the better part of an hour to reprogramme the navi-comp. During that time, Vila and Avon were attempting to access the onboard computer without it shutting down. The trouble was, every time they tried to hack the system files the computer interpreted it as some form of corruptive virus attacking the entire system and would immediately shutdown and reboot.

Jenna paused for a moment, the dust panel still unlatched from the front of the navi-comp, her work all but forgotten. She tapped the phasic-wrench thoughtfully against her thigh as she thought the idea through. 'I think there might be a way around this,' she said. 'If I'm right we can use the transmitter signal to cancel out the transponder altogether. That way we won't have to touch the computer systems.'

'Do you really know what you're talking about or are you just trying to impress me?' Vila asked.

There was silence for a handful of seconds. Then, at last, Avon's head emerged from the place it had been buried for the past 60 minutes – the open panel beneath the computer terminal – his face smudged with dust and machine oil. 'That would mean boosting the signal beyond the tolerance level of the equipment, it might not last very long. Judging by the age of the ship, it's possible the whole transmitter array could short out within minutes, possibly less.'

'It still might be long enough to confuse the pursuit ships,' said Jenna. 'Or at least convince them that we're no longer on the *Dionysus.*'

Avon considered this, although admittedly not for long. 'Worth a try, particularly as we're running out of time and options.'

Jenna nodded. 'What have we got to lose?'

'Oh, apart from our lives,' Vila returned sarcastically. 'Nothing at all, really.'

Blake looked down at the small, black box in front of him and thought, 'So this is the CCT, is it? This is what so many members of the Freedom Party died to protect?'

They'd returned to the ops-room, only this time Tobin had switched on the narrow strip lighting that ran the entire length of the walls, completely encircling the room, and now Blake was able to see the equipment properly. He had to admit it was much more impressive than he had first thought. Most of it was new, or at least well looked after by its previous owner, and each component appeared to be compatible with the neighbouring one. Even those pieces that so obviously didn't match had been expertly joined together using industrial shunt-rig connectors and channelled through power converters.

Everything in the room was connected up to the Centralised

Computer Terminal, which sat almost dead centre of a large hexagonal control unit to one side of the main entrance. The entire room was set up like some vast network library, so that every piece of information was routed into the CCT, where it was stored until needed. All the information could then be flashed across to the bank of computer terminals on the far wall at the touch of a button.

Blake turned slowly, taking in the rest of the room. His eye was suddenly caught by Tobin, who sat over by the comms desk regarding Orac closely, a look of almost comic perplexity on his face.

'Is that it?'

Blake's words appeared to burst some fragile bubble of thought, dragging Tobin back into the room with a start. He glanced up towards the CCT where the rebel leader stood.

'Sorry?' he said and smiled apologetically.

'You're thinking "Is that it? Is that really the mighty supercomputer Orac?"' said Blake. 'Don't worry, most people do. I've been thinking something similar about the equipment in this room.'

All perplexity had vanished from Tobin's face now, replaced by a look of almost abject fascination. 'What's it doing?'

'I've asked Orac to copy all the files you've been pulling from the Federation archives over the past few years,' Blake said. 'I'm hoping that there might be one or two files stored in your database that no longer exist in the Federation's central computer, things they might have deleted some time after you copied them.'

'There really isn't anything in there relating to Archangel,' Tobin told him. 'I've run a thorough check of the files, trust me.' He dropped his eyes to the ground, embarrassed by his own choice of words. 'What I mean is, I wasn't lying to you about that.'

Blake said, 'I know. I'd already guessed that much.'

'Then what are you looking for?' asked Tobin.

'Information on the Callidus system,' Blake said. 'Anything that Orac can find. Ever since you gave me that name and we intercepted that transmission…' Blake stopped and looked at Tobin. 'Since that transmission was aimed at us, I've been trying to figure out why it seemed so familiar to me, where I'd heard it before. Well, it finally came to me, while we were sitting in the grass on that hillside.

'Five years ago, at one of the Freedom Party meetings, a young cyberneticist I'd never met before called Kodyn Tam was introduced to me. He said that he'd been approached by the Federation to work on a new project, and when he declined they'd made it very clear that they weren't prepared to take no for an answer. Kodyn told me that they'd threatened his family and he wanted out of the Dome – in fact he wanted to get off Earth altogether.

'He actually revealed very little about the details of the project they wanted him to work on, except that they'd referred to it as Archangel and it had something to do with the propulsion system for a new class of pursuit ship,' Blake said. 'But there was something about the project that Kodyn didn't like, found distasteful even. He said that what they were asking him to do felt…wrong.'

'What were they asking him to do?'

Blake shrugged. 'He didn't say and I didn't ask. He just told me that he hadn't trained for all those years for his skills to be used for something as twisted as that.' Blake nodded at the memory. 'That was the word he used – twisted.'

'Tam was a cybernetic engineer, right?' asked Tobin.

Blake nodded. 'One of the best. Studied under Calvino.'

'But all this was some time ago,' Tobin said. 'Archangel has been shut down for at least three years. If you do find any information on the project what good will it do you now?'

'Because I'm not convinced that Archangel is as dead and buried as the Federation would like us to believe,' said Blake, glancing across at Orac. 'In fact I'm almost certain that someone is trying to start the project up again.' His eyes flicked momentarily back to Tobin. 'Only this time it's without the High Council's knowledge. I think that whoever it is will be there, at the Callidus system. Project Archangel began there five years ago and I think that's where it's starting again. I need to find out who's behind all this and stop them, before innocent people start dying all over again.'

artefact[4]

Malcus hated the shipyards, always had. Even as a boy, when his father had brought him here with his little sister Fraya, he hadn't enjoyed it.

It was no secret that his father had wished his children to be bitten by the engineering bug too, had hoped that perhaps one day a visit out to these immense web-like structures orbiting Callidus IX would inspire them both to follow in their father's footsteps and enrol in the Federation's Space Engineering Program.

But Malcus had always found the shipyards mind-numbingly dull and regarded his occasional visits there as something to be endured rather than looked forward to. And yet, despite this, he had always kept those thoughts and feelings to himself, never sharing them with anyone, not his friends nor his sister – and especially not his father. Malcus knew that the truth would have devastated him, had he known it.

And so, Malcus had pretended to be delighted whenever his father had returned home, announcing that he had arranged passage for the three of them on a cargo-hauler the following day, to take them out to the Callidus system.

Malcus had hated the cargo-haulers too: the way they creaked and groaned with every movement, the way the deck-plates would vibrate and shift beneath his feet whenever they made planetfall, but most of all he had hated the smell. That stomach-churning mix of sweat and machine oil and rotting flesh. The shipyards were no better.

So little has changed over the years, Malcus thought.

These memories came back to him as he rode the lift up to the dry dock, where the Stinger prototype was waiting to be connected up to the advanced mutoid-thing... Wait, what were they calling them now?

He glanced down at the small electronic device in his hand and scanned the project manifest again. *Archangels.* That was it, that was what the test subjects were being referred to now: Archangels.

Calling it the Advanced Mutoid Programme had proved unpopular, particularly with the grunts in Space Command. They'd taken to nicknaming it The Freakshow. It had started out as a joke amongst the officers in the mess halls, but it wasn't long before they were openly referring to it as such in official communiqués. Very soon the upper echelons of Space Command had become involved, and an order came down from Space Commander Velkin himself, stating that he personally would discipline anyone caught using the name in public, either in conversation or over an official Federation communications frequency. Not long after that the name was changed to Project Archangel.

Malcus scrolled down through the information until he found the details he required:

Name:	Sheya Tobin
Designation:	Test Subject: Two (of Seven)
Codename:	Raphael
Sex:	Male
Age:	Twenty-Four (24)
Birthplace:	Gamma Aquilus II (Alpha Colony)

And that was all the information there was on the subject. Malcus cycled through the attached folders, looking for the background notes, but there was no more. He typed in 'Additional Information' and thumbed the search button. No results. He tried altering the search pattern a little, cross-referencing it with the Archangel tab, still nothing.

By the time he'd reached the dry dock platform, 15 minutes later, he'd given up on the data search altogether; the electronic device had been returned to his overall pocket and he was flicking idly through the day's itinerary instead.

Beran was waiting for him at the other end of the walkway, dabbing at his face and neck with a handkerchief, his bald pate glowing wetly in the bone-white glare of the arc lamps that hung from the ceiling. The little man shuffled towards Malcus, a mixture of relief and annoyance wrestling for control of his features.

'You're late,' he squeaked. 'The Advancement is already here. They smuggled it through the side airlock an hour ago.'

Malcus tapped his overall pocket, indicating the small electronic device housed within. 'Archangel.'

'Eh?' Beran's head jerked around. He peered distrustfully up at his companion. 'What are you talking about?'

'Memo from the Presidential Office.' Malcus raised an eyebrow at the little man. 'We don't call them Advancements anymore. Or Freaks, Advanced Mutoids, Constructs or Augments, come to that. They're called Archangels now.'

Colour suddenly sprang to Beran's cheeks and the handkerchief appeared once more, fluttering across his throat and chin. 'Since when?'

'Since two days ago,' Malcus told him. 'You really must check your info-feed more often.'

In answer Beran pointed across the dry dock to where the prototype was berthed. 'I don't have time for that nonsense, I've been too busy.'

The ship took Malcus by surprise. He'd thought he'd known what it was going to look like – he'd seen the original 3D schematics and approved most of the upgrades – but he had no idea that it would look so... *powerful.*

For a start they'd built up the aft section – obviously to allow the experimental drive system to be grafted into the existing engine housing – but with the new tail fins and the venting grills there was virtually nothing recognisable left of the original Type 1 pursuit ship chassis. And with the new weapon system they'd placed at the front, just below the fuselage, the thing reminded him of some vicious, powerfully-built creature – an ugly great leviathan from the darkest depths of the ocean. It was a fanciful image, but one that disturbed Malcus nevertheless.

'Looks to me like they've modified the tail section a little from the original blueprints,' Malcus said, a little stunned. 'I wouldn't mind getting a closer look at that thing before proceedings get underway.'

Beran shook his head. 'No time for that now. You're an hour late as it is and I've delayed them for as long as I can. You'll have to wait until after the demonstration.' He shrugged, then added as an afterthought, 'It's your own fault. I told you to get here on time, didn't I?'

'All right, all right.' Malcus flapped a hand at the little man, as though he were some kind of irritating insect buzzing around him. 'A little less of the "I told you so" if you don't mind. Let's go and get ourselves front row seats, shall we?'

Malcus smiled as his old friend scuttled off across the dry dock, muttering miserably beneath his breath. He took one last look at the Stinger, the smile slipping slowly from his face, then he turned and headed after Beran.

The observation lounge was virtually empty when they arrived, so they chose a couple of seats at the front, away from the small gathering of admin types who were collecting along the back row. One of them caught Malcus's eye as he wandered down the aisle, offering him a brisk but pleasant nod, before turning back to the conversation.

Desk pilots from the Presidential Office, Malcus thought, eyeing their crisp, unblemished white tunics and soft, well-manicured hands with obvious distaste. *Probably the first time they've ventured outside the Terran system.*

Malcus noted that the observation lounge was actually a basic MK III box-kit with two, tall cantilever legs bolted on, in order to raise it further above the platform. The engineers had shoved it untidily up against the wall, at the very edge of the platform, probably so that it could overlook the main testing area without getting in the way too much.

On the platform below, the technical crew were starting to assemble, prompting Malcus to lean forward and power up the communication panel.

'I do hope they haven't given the job of moderator to that fool Sherma again,' Malcus said. 'He made such a hash of things last time.'

Beran sniffed noisily, rubbing at his nose with the handkerchief as he peered around the observation lounge. 'It'll either be him or Moola the Mumbler. I can never understand a damn word that idiot utters.'

In a matter of minutes, the seats around them had begun to fill up. A group of five officials from the Administration Committee joined them on the front row, prompting the two men to shuffle along a bit until there was enough room for the small party to be seated.

Malcus settled himself into the new seat, surreptitiously glancing sideways at the newcomers, careful not to make it too obvious that he was looking at them. After a moment or two he leant casually on the arm of his chair, inclining his head until his mouth was near Beran's ear.

'Be on your best behaviour, Beran, my old friend,' he whispered. 'If I'm not mistaken that's Councillor Alexei sitting at the end of our row.'

Beran's eyes widened then began to twitch wildly, as though he were trying to stop himself from glancing over.

'You never told me that the President would be sending his number one adviser to this little party,' Malcus said. 'Shame on you, Beran. If I'd have known she was coming then I would have probably arrived on this miserable junk pile on time.'

'I never took you for a brown nose, Malcus,' Beran hissed from the side of his mouth.

When everything was ready they brought the Archangel out onto the platform, escorted between two armed troopers. Several people sitting in the observation lounge actually gasped, and Malcus found himself unconsciously leaning forward in his seat, as though this would somehow afford him a better view of the upgraded human.

To his left a voice said, 'It doesn't look much like a mutoid to me.'

It belonged to Councillor Alexei. Malcus noticed that she too was leaning expectantly on the edge of her seat, her gloved hands gripping the support railing in front of her a little too tightly. A number of people murmured their agreement, but none dared speak nor look away from the scene that was unfolding on the platform below. And for a while there was a long, heavy silence.

The Archangel had been brought forward then manoeuvred around to the starboard side of the ship where it was met by two of the technical crew. Malcus couldn't help but notice that the two men were wearing protective masks that covered their mouths and noses.

It took a little time for them to connect up the Archangel, strapping it securely into the Stinger's modified cockpit, and by the time they emerged back out onto the platform the small gathering of scientists and Administration officials collected inside the observation lounge was beginning to grow impatient.

One of the technicians gave a thumbs-up and both men trotted off across the dry dock in the direction of the control tower. As soon as they were clear, the Stinger's engines roared into life and the undercarriage began to slowly inch its way off the ground, the air beneath its takeoff vents rippling as though someone had dipped a finger into a puddle of rainwater.

Malcus knew that something was wrong almost immediately, even when others around him started to applaud. It wasn't anything he could have put his finger on, not at first. All he knew was that the craft was holding itself all wrong.

The ship was circling slowly as though it was looking for something, swinging its nose around in an arc, until it finally came to rest facing the large, panoramic window of the observation lounge. From here, Malcus could clearly see the pilot through the craft's reinforced plexi-glass window, could see its white, featureless eyes staring out in his direction.

The Archangel was looking at him, directly at *him*, Malcus was sure of it; goose bumps crept suddenly up his spine, reaching out for the nape of his neck. Why had no-one else noticed this? He glanced about him, turning his head this way and that, but everyone else seemed relaxed; some were even beginning to chat amongst themselves as though they had already lost interest in the demonstration.

So when the Stinger Class assault ship suddenly flicked on its retro-burners and hurtled towards the observation lounge at a little under Time Distort Three absolutely no-one was expecting it – except, maybe, for Senior Technician Malcus.

The resulting explosion completely obliterated the dry dock, killing everyone instantly, and fracturing the support-struts on the west wing of Shipyard B. Fires spread along the structure, destroying thirty-four transporters and killing more than five hundred men and women.

News of the disaster was suppressed by the High Council and the Callidus shipyards were abandoned for good – something that would have pleased Malcus no end, had he lived.

It was reported that all personnel had died in a civil transporter crash on their way back to the Terran system. The footage of the blazing wreckage shown on the vid-casts was of the passenger ship *Rohilla*, which had crashed shipping families out to the new colonies eight years earlier, but no one noticed.

Four days later, project Archangel was shut down and all files referring to it removed from central archives.

CHAPTER TEN

Jenna had no idea how long the signal would be active for; it really all depended on whether the transmitter array could cope with the high volume of power. The problem was, there was no way for her to test it. If she was to try, and the array blew during the trial run, then it'd take the three of them another two hours just to fit a new set of breakers.

'We've retuned the ship's onboard distress beacon so that it now transmits at the same frequency as the device buried in Kodyn's chest. Some of the pulse settings are a little out, but it should be near enough to convince the pursuit ships that it's the original transmitter signal,' Jenna explained. 'The only problem is, we can't alter the ship's ID tag. Every time we try to access the transponder codes the computer thinks it's being attacked and shuts down. So we've had to think around the problem.'

Blake didn't seem to be comforted by her words. 'I'm sure you've done your best,' he said, with a frown.

'It's far from perfect, I'm afraid, but it's the only way we've found of masking the transponder signal,' Jenna said.

'If the Federation ships pick up the new transponder ID they'll assume that Kodyn has jumped ship at the *Dionysus*,' said Avon. 'Then they'd start scanning the sector for the *Liberator*'s energy signature and we'd be back to square one.'

'But if we boost the distress beacon's signal until its power output is so great that it blankets all other transmissions...' Jenna shrugged. 'There's a good chance that they'll think they're still following Kodyn's signal aboard the *Liberator*.'

It wasn't quite the foolproof plan that Blake had hoped for, but it might still work. 'Is there a possibility that they could still identify the craft's transponder codes?'

Avon nodded slowly. 'It will take them a while to isolate the relevant pulse beneath all the confusion, but it could be done.'

'By then we'll be long gone and our energy trail should have dissipated,' said Jenna. 'At least, that's the theory.'

As they spoke Jenna had been cycling up the shuttlepod's engines while disconnecting all superfluous systems from the main power grid, including life support – the hope being that the less power feeding off the ship's grid, the less chance the array had of overloading immediately and giving the game away.

She punched the new co-ordinates into the autodrive systems and programmed the engines to fire in two minutes. Admittedly Jenna would have been happier had they been given a little more time to get clear of the landing pad, but two minutes was the maximum time offered by the booster controls – they'd just have to make do.

Jenna ushered Blake and Avon out of the cramped shuttlepod interior and down onto the landing pad, ducking under the craft's blunt, stubby nosecone as they ran back across the hanger bay towards the flight control station. Behind them the whining roar of the take-off jets was reaching an almost unbearable pitch, prompting them to quicken their pace as they covered the remaining few yards to the sanctuary of the control station.

They just made it inside as the huge metal doors on the far side of the hanger began to spiral slowly open, revealing cold, starless space beyond. The shuttlepod was starting to rotate now, its retros spinning around in their direction as the craft quickly aligned itself with the hanger doors.

They watched the small craft as it taxied steadily across the deck and disappeared out into the darkness. For a while the afterburn from the shuttlepod's retros was like a bright, burning star against the black, then it banked sharply to starboard and vanished.

'This had better work, Blake, or I'm going to have every Federation assault trooper in the sector suddenly descending on this platform,' Tobin said.

'It'll work, trust me,' Blake told him, but Jenna caught the brief troubled look that accompanied his words.

'This place is supposed to be neutral,' Tobin whined, obviously noticing the look too. 'The Federation leave us alone on the understanding that we don't get involved.'

It was a damn stupid thing to say, and Jenna could tell that Tobin knew it the moment the words were out of his mouth. Colour sprang to his cheeks and he dropped his eyes to the floor.

'I had no choice in what I did before, I told you that. I've come clean with you about what happened and now I just want to be left out of this.'

Behind him Avon said, 'You're deluding yourself if you believe that you can stay out of this.'

Blake thumbed the communication button on his teleport bracelet. '*Liberator*, this is Blake. We're ready to come aboard.' He severed the connection quickly, then glanced across at Tobin. 'Avon's right, sooner or later you're going to have to make a choice. I hope you make the right one, my old friend.'

And then Blake and his friends were gone, leaving Tobin to his thoughts.

'Do you trust him?' Avon asked, once they were back on board the *Liberator*.

'No,.' Blake admitted, sadly. 'There's something he's still not telling us. Perhaps Travis still has a hold over him.' He thought about it for a moment, before adding, 'But it makes no difference, we're still going to the Callidus system.'

'Why?' Jenna asked, in surprise.

'Because I don't think *Travis* is the one trying to restart Project Archangel,' Blake said. 'I don't think he knows much about it, he was just using it as bait to get us to Sigma Minor so he could get his hands on the *Liberator*.' He paused. 'But *I'm* positive that Archangel is real and that someone is trying to restart it. And we can't afford to let that happen. I think we'll find whoever it is there at the Callidus system. I'm willing to stake my life on it.'

'The question is are we willing to stake *our* lives on it?' Avon asked him coldly.

'What about Kodyn?' asked Jenna.

'I think we've got everything we're going to get from him.' said Blake. 'He needs time to rest, to recuperate. He's not going to get that where we're going. We'll have to leave him here.'

When the doctor returned to the medical suite later in the day, the medibot was out of its charging unit and flopping helplessly on the floor in the corner of the room, obviously in some distress.

He pulled the remote control device from his pocket and clicked the recall button.

In response the medibot emitted an abrupt string of high-pitched chirrups, but other than that there was no change in the machine's behaviour. The doctor thumbed the button half a dozen more times in rapid succession but still it did no good.

At first the doctor had assumed that the medibot had got itself stuck, that it had somehow rolled over onto its back and was unable to right itself again, like a turtle. But on closer inspection he found that the machine had been deliberately damaged. Someone had picked it up and swung it forcibly against the wall, virtually splitting the carapace from end to end.

Once more the doctor aimed the small control device at the medibot, ordering it to power down so that he could handle it without getting a neutronic shock. Again it took him several attempts, but in the end the pulse finally made it through the machine's damaged receptors and its energy core began to power down.

He waited until he thought it was safe then prodded it cautiously with the toe of his boot. As if in answer the machine fizzed and crackled, then the lights along its outer casing blinked off and it eventually fell still and silent.

The doctor picked it up and placed it on a nearby table, its innards rattling alarmingly as it shifted in his hands. The thing sounded like it was full of large, heavy ball bearings.

He leaned further forwards, trying to peer into the cracked shell of the machine, assessing the damage. *I may know next to nothing about advanced robotics,* the doctor thought with a sigh, *but even I can see that this thing is a lost cause.*

The machine had been charging when he'd left it, so whoever had come in must have ripped it from its wall unit. He glanced across at the far wall, expecting to see the charging unit torn from its housing, but it wasn't, it was still there in one piece.

Small mercies, he thought sourly.

That's when he noticed that the bed was empty and the patient was nowhere to be seen.

He dropped what was left of the medibot onto the table and scuttled over to the empty bed. The covers had been tossed back into a heap in the middle which, from the doorway, had made it look like there was still someone in it.

Without thinking he reached for the panel on the wall above the bed and slammed the palm of his hand against the security button.

By the time the orderlies arrived, the medibot was all but forgotten.

It would be another six hours before they realised that several pieces of its power core were missing.

Tobin was not good at waiting. He'd sent the communication off over an hour ago (four words, just as they'd agreed: *The games have begun*) but so far he still hadn't received an acknowledgement.

This time he'd not bothered going all the way down to the ops-room. Instead, he'd ordered that all communications be channelled into his private office, and he sat staring out of the viewing window, watching the service shuttlepods ferrying the visitors back and forth.

Today he really didn't feel like doing the meet and greets. Standing up in front of all those happy, expectant faces, going through the usually spiel of how he hoped they'd enjoy their stay on the platform, and that all their dreams, all their fantasies – no matter how depraved – were about to come true here on the *Dionysus.*

The communicator on his desk bleeped softly and Tobin sat up quickly in his chair, the latest batch of visitors suddenly forgotten. He slammed a palm down onto the *answer* button.

'Director Tobin.' He tried to make his voice sound as calm as possible.

'There's an outside communiqué for you, sir. Caller didn't give a name, just said it was urgent and you'd know what it was about.'

'Yes, I've been expecting it,' said Tobin. 'Patch them through please, Gira.' He snapped the control to *off*, but then something seemed to suddenly occur to him, and he opened the channel again. 'Oh and Gira, I don't want to be disturbed for a while. I've got one or two personal matters to attend to. In fact, can you ask Jarvell to cover my meet and greet for the next visitor induction, please?'

'Jarvell is off-platform at the moment, sir. Won't be back for another 72 hours. I think Kimba is on downtime today, she might be free. I could call and ask.'

But Tobin was no longer listening. Instead his eyes were on the steadily blinking light to the left of the communication panel, the one that reminded him that there was someone waiting to speak to him on the other channel.

'That's great,' he said vaguely. 'I'll leave that to you then, shall I?' And he cut the line. His hand hovered above the panel for a while, his fingers clenching and flexing as he stared silently at the flashing light, steeling himself for the conversation that was to follow. After a moment or two he reached forward and opened the channel. 'This is Director Tobin.'

'Ah, at last. For a minute there I was beginning to think that you had forgotten me. If I didn't know you better, Tobin, I would have said that you did it on purpose.'

The voice may have sounded playful but Tobin was no fool; he was well aware of the implications that lay beneath its tone. 'My apologies. I was sorting out a few mundane work matters, things that needed my immediate attention. But I am here now.' He paused, before adding unnecessarily, 'You got my message?'

The voice sighed at the stupidity of the question. *'Obviously. I trust everything went well?'*

'I think so, yes. At least he seemed to believe my story – after I let him threaten me for a while.' Tobin smiled. 'I even let that uncultured criminal Avon hit me a few times, just for effect.'

'Showing initiative. I like that.' And there did appear to be a tinge of genuine pleasure in the voice. *'A pity you're no longer with us, we could do with a few more like you in Space Command at the moment.'*

Tobin chose to ignore that. 'As you predicted he used that box-thing of his to copy all the archive files, then took them back to his ship. He seemed happy with the information I could give him.'

'Excellent. And you gave him Travis's name? That bit was very important.'

Tobin nodded. 'Yes, I told him. And it's true, Travis *did* give me that data slug, but that was such a long time ago now, before he went on the run. He knew that Blake would come here to the *Dionysus* eventually for my help. All Travis wanted was for me to hand over the slug, then let him know when it was done so he could prepare an ambush. He just wanted Blake and the *Liberator*, that was all.'

'I assure you, Tobin, my intentions are the same. I have merely... tweaked the plan a little. That fool Travis failed to understand the implications of the name Kodyn Tam. I did not. That is why I have adjusted the plan accordingly. Using their names makes things much more... tempting for Blake.'

Tobin decided to remain silent.

'What about the transmitting device inside Tam?'

'He had one of our doctors disable it. It was the only way they could shut it off without killing him.'

'But my ships are still tracking the signal.'

'Blake had one of his women alter the distress beacon on a shuttlepod so that it would pulse on a similar frequency.'

'How remarkably inventive of him.' The voice was impressed. *'I've obviously been underestimating Blake's tenacity all this time. Where is he now?'*

'Back onboard his ship. They are hiding somewhere nearby, waiting for your pursuit ships to pass out of range.' Tobin said.

'Then I shall tell my fleet captain to remain on course with the signal. Once I have received a further signal that Blake is on the move I will have them alter course and follow beyond detector range.'

Tobin drummed his fingers on the desk impatiently; the conversation was not going quite the way he had planned. 'Wait a minute – what further signal? That was not our agreement.' He jabbed a finger at the communication panel. 'You said there was only one more thing that you needed me to do and after that our bargain would be complete.'

'Ah, yes, that. I'm afraid I won't be able to uphold my end of the deal after all.'

'What? I don't understand.' Fear began to claw at Tobin then. It hung around him like a thick pall of mist. 'You promised me that you would do everything you could to get my son back.'

'I did say that, you're absolutely right. But unfortunately I was lying.' The voice sounded amused. *'You see, your son is dead, Tobin. He died a couple of years ago.'*

The news arrived like a backhand to his face. Tobin's first instinct was to stand up and leave the room, to get away from the cruel, mocking voice on the other end of the communicator, but his legs refused to obey him. He fell back down again into his chair and stared at the blazing white light on the communication panel for a long while. His lips flapped silently as though all words had become lodged in his throat. He felt ridiculous, like a fish that had been dragged out of the water and was now gasping uselessly at the air, waiting for death.

'He's... dead?' Tobin managed to jerk out at last. 'How?'

'Does that really matter now?' the voice asked.

'I need to know if my son suffered,' Tobin pleaded. 'Was it quick, when the end came?'

There was a silence, as though the voice at the other end of the open channel was considering whether to lie to him or not.

Finally the voice told him, *'No, it wasn't quick. From what I can gather your son died in a great deal of agony. There was nothing our cyberneticists could do for him.'*

'Cyberneticists?' Tobin was confused. 'I don't understand. You said that he was on Pharrox...'

'Another lie. As was my promise that I would let you live, I'm afraid.' The voice chuckled delightedly. *'I've hardly been truthful with you at all really, have I?'*

Tobin looked up as the side door to his office clanked open. Two Federation troopers stepped briskly in from the room beyond, visors obscuring their faces, weapons raised and levelled in his direction. For a second or two he didn't react, just sat there glaring across at his two new guests as though they were nothing more than some minor irritant interrupting his private conversation.

Slowly Tobin turned back to the communication panel. 'What about the signal?'

'Signal?'

'You said you wanted me to inform you when Blake was on the move again.' Tobin said.

'A misunderstanding on your part,' came the answer. *'A signal will be sent, but not by you. The two gentlemen who have just joined you will be quite capable of transmitting the signal, when the time comes.'*

One of the troopers stepped closer, the muzzle of his gun now level with Tobin's head.

'And now our business is concluded. But first I would like to thank you, Tobin, for all you've done in helping me capture Blake and his crew. I couldn't have done it without you. Fleet Captain, you may proceed.'

The trooper only fired a single shot; it was all that was needed. Tobin was killed instantly. The trooper had done this kind of thing before, hundreds of times, quelling dozens of civilian uprisings while honing his execution skills. The shot entered the skull just above the bridge of the nose, spraying fragments of bone and brain across the viewing window behind him. Tobin spasmed only once, before falling onto the desk.

The troopers dragged the body from the chair and dumped it over in the corner before quickly locking both doors. After that they settled down to wait for Blake to make his move.

PART THREE
Project Archangel

CHAPTER ELEVEN

The *Liberator* drifted silently amongst the ancient dust and rocks of Gamma Xenos III's planetary rings. Its life support and drive systems had been cycled down to bare minimum and now it was just another piece of space flotsam floating amongst the lifeless debris that circled the blue gas giant. Every now and then small correctional jets along its port and starboard flanks would splutter into life, pushing the ship out of harm's way whenever a jagged splinter of ice or large chunk of rock wandered dangerously close.

It was a trick that Jenna had picked up from her days as a smuggler; it had been a bit of a favourite with an old colleague of hers called Virna. She told Vila that she always referred to it as silent running. Vila informed her that he had a much better and far more accurate name for it – certain death.

What bothered Vila was the close proximity of thousands of huge lumps of deadly rock. No, *actually* what bothered Vila *most* was the fact that the *Liberator* had its drive systems and weapon systems all but switched off and was pretty much drifting helplessly without engines or a means of defence... that *and* the close proximity of thousands of huge lumps of deadly rock. Both scenarios were completely insane in Vila's eyes, but to combine the two.... he had yet to invent a suitable adjective that best summed up just how insane this situation actually was.

'Relax, Vila,' Blake had told him. 'We're totally safe. Nothing is going to hit us.'

'And even if something did, with the force wall powered down we wouldn't feel a thing, we'd be vaporised instantly,' Avon added with a smile.

'You're only saying that to cheer me up.' Vila finished off the adrenalin and soma in one, long gulp, then immediately refilled his glass. This time he didn't stop pouring until the liquid was almost overflowing.

On the table in front of him, Orac began to whirr that little bit louder, indicating that he was about to impart something of great importance which, as far as Vila was aware, seemed to be anything and everything it had to say. 'Federation ships are now passing the

Dionysus platform at a distance of 3,000 spacials, as yet no deviation has been detected. Present course and speed would suggest that they are in pursuit of the shuttlepod.'

Vila was obviously delighted by this and raised his glass in salute towards Orac. 'Great. Does that mean we can get out of here now?'

Blake shook his head. 'Not until they're far enough away.' He turned, glancing across at the oval panel on the far wall. 'Zen, how long until we're out of range of the Federation ships' detectors?'

Lights moved along the surface of the panel. 'AT PRESENT SPEED AND COURSE, *LIBERATOR* WILL BE OUT OF DETECTOR RANGE IN 38 MINUTES AND 27 SECONDS.'

'Let's hope that they don't catch up with the shuttlepod before then.' Cally said.

'I don't think that will happen,' Avon told her.

Cally nodded, looking pleased by this news. 'That is good to hear.'

'It's far more likely that the transmitter array will have blown long before they catch up with it,' Avon said.

It wasn't the clearest of images, but it was the best that Orac said he could find in the archives. Even so, the object was still easily identifiable.

At first it looked like a series of circular cracks on the northern hemisphere of the planet, as though the world were an egg and something had punctured and cracked its shell. But then, as Orac began to zoom in, it started to look more like a vast, silver web that had been spun by some giant, mutant spider 1,000 spacials above the planet's surface. Of course it was neither. Exactly what it was became clear the moment the vid-clip was at full magnification.

Up close the structure was really quite mundane, not to mention ugly. Its reinforced carbo-steel support struts were blackened by years of exhaust energy from the retro-burners of the ships that had been launched from its skeletal innards.

'The great Callidus shipyards,' Blake announced, somewhat grandly. Vila was almost disappointed. 'That's it? An abandoned shipyard? That's what all the fuss has been about? That... dead, blackened monstrosity is Archangel?'

'Don't be stupid, Vila,' Jenna snapped.

'The lair of the great metal spider god.'

Although Cally's words were softly spoken, they had been loud enough for everyone on the flight deck to hear them. It took her a moment or two to realise that all conversation had stopped and every pair of eyes was looking in her direction.

Blake raised an inquisitive eyebrow. 'Is there something you want to share with the rest of us?'

'Actually, I'm not sure I want to hear about it,' Vila said under his breath.

'It was something my father told us when we were very young. I had always assumed that it was a children's story – a fiction designed to be used as a warning to children, like the Spirits of the M'garta or the Thaarn.' Cally nodded towards the viewscreen. 'The story told of a great metal spider god who spun a web so vast that it circled an entire planet. Ahmak, the greatest of all Auron warriors was sent to talk to the spider god and beg for the release of the people of the planet that she had imprisoned.'

'Let me guess,' said Vila. 'The spider god wasn't quite as understanding as the Aurons had hoped?'

Cally shook her head. 'Ahmak was captured and eaten by the spider god.'

A shiver of fear ran down Vila's spine. He was right, he really didn't want to hear that story.

'Fairy stories,' said Orac, 'and totally immaterial to the matter in hand. Exactly the type of reason why the Callidus shipyards have been the subject of superstition and rumour for most of their working life, even amongst the Federation pilots themselves. Everything that was done there was highly classified. Even movement in and out of the sector was strictly limited to shipyard personnel.'

'So no one knows what work went on there, and we're still no nearer an explanation as to why the place was shut down,' said Vila, gloomily. 'Great, thanks Orac.'

'Use your eyes, Vila.' Blake gestured towards the image on the viewscreen. 'Isn't it obvious why they shut the place down? An explosion on that scale would have wiped out the central core of the complex. I'm surprised Tobin couldn't find any data in the archives about this.'

'Just because he was unable to do so does not mean that the data was not there for him to find,' Orac said. 'Only that he did not have the advantage of an advanced computer system like me to help him.'

'If you're waiting for a round of applause I'm afraid you're going to be disappointed.' Avon said. 'If you've found something just tell us.'

'I have managed to find evidence within the Federation archive files I obtained from his computer. Evidence of the kind of work that was going on inside the shipyards.

'It appears that work began five years ago on a new Stinger Class pursuit ship, one that would be capable of achieving speeds in excess of Time Distort 30. The ship was equipped with a direct neural-feed drive system, which meant that, once the Federation had begun mass production, an entire flotilla of such vessels could theoretically be gridlinked to a central flagship computer guaranteeing a precise co-ordinated attack response. Taking such decisions out of the hands of human pilots would mean a faster, more accurate response time with an almost zero percent probability of error. But an accident three years ago involving a prototype model caused the whole structure of the shipyards to be declared unsafe and the complex was soon evacuated and shut down.

'Scans suggest that the ship may have been armed with phasium-tipped warheads, which may account for the widespread structural damage. A massive fire tore through the shipyards, killing hundreds of people and buckling most of the support struts on the west wing of the structure. They've not been used since.'

There was silence for a while, as everyone tried to process the implications of what Orac had just said.

Obviously Vila arrived at his usual conclusions, namely that it meant certain death for him. 'So why are we going there exactly?' he said at last.

'Because we think that Project Archangel is being restarted by someone,' said Blake. 'And we need to put a stop to it. Fast.'

Avon said, 'There is one obvious question that no-one has bothered to ask yet.'

'I've a feeling that you're about to ask it, though,' Blake said with a smile.

'Why stop the experiments?' Avon asked.

'Because there was an accident that cost hundreds of lives?' Jenna offered.

Avon shook his head. 'But why should that stop the experiments? A few minor teething troubles have never stopped them before. What are a few hundred lives to the Federation?'

'Minor teething troubles?' Vila said incredulously. 'You consider the death of everyone in the shipyards as "minor teething troubles"?'

'That wasn't what Avon said, Vila,' said Cally.

'Avon's quite right,' said Blake with a frown. 'For a project as important as this, that's *exactly* how the Federation would regard those deaths: nothing more than a temporary setback, an inconvenience. If they had a ship that could reach such speeds – no, if they had an entire fleet of ships… They'd be unstoppable.'

'They could reach the outer worlds in a matter of hours,' Avon said. 'Civil uprisings would be squashed before they had even properly begun.'

'They'd even go after the smugglers on the outer rim, stop the supply line to the main dissident groups,' said Jenna. 'With ships like that the Federation could do anything they liked. No-one would be able to outrun them.'

'Not even the *Liberator*,' said Vila. And the thought unnerved him.

'Which leads me to ask the question again,' said Avon. 'Why stop the experiments?'

Blake considered his colleague's question for a brief moment before turning very slowly back towards the viewscreen, pointing up at the image of the dark and silent shipyards. 'I've really no idea. But I have a feeling that these shipyards may be where all the answers lie.' Blake glanced away from the screen, looking at each of his crewmates in turn. 'Shall we go and look?'

artefact[5]

ADMINISTRATION BUILDING – EARTH.

Archive File: 20-09/077
Format: Datacube
Subject: Test Subjects, deaths of
Status: Encrypted (Eyes Only)

Scene - Committee Room.

[The lights are turned down and most of the room is in darkness. The only light comes from the vid-screen on the far wall. The film is grainy and a little out of focus. We see bodies suspended from the ceiling by tubes and wires, followed by men in white, sterile uniforms poking around inside bloody cadavers lying on featureless slabs of metal. After a while the film comes to an end and the lights snap on. Four people – two men and two women – sit around a large, semi-circular table; each has a terminal screen in front of them. These are Project Supervisor BRECK, Councillors ABNER and GYST, and Secretary RONTANE.]

GYST: [after a long silence] There were no survivors?

BRECK: None.

GYST: Do we have a full explanation yet as to why this happened?

BRECK: We have a pretty good idea. However Dr Judd's team is currently looking into the matter in some depth, so we should have a full report by the end of the week.

RONTANE: Keldo said that there would be safeguards put into place, to stop this kind of thing from happening.

BRECK: He did. But from what I can gather the safeguards just didn't work in this instance.

ABNER: According to Keldo's initial report, the problem was neurological.

BRECK: That is correct, yes.

ABNER: So, the test subjects rejected the implants?

BRECK: In a way, yes, but the problem goes much deeper than that. As I say it's still early days yet but it looks as if the real cause may stem from the Network itself.

ABNER: The Network?

BRECK: More specifically, its gridlink software.

GYST: This was also a problem in the original prototypes, yes?

BRECK: That is correct, although Pellas tried to compensate for the problem by introducing a neural-feed interface, which he had implanted at the top of each of the subjects' spinal cords.

RONTANE: Neural-feed interface?

BRECK: In layman's terms the neural-feed interface is what links the subjects' minds to the ship's guidance systems. Think of it as a kind of power transformer, only instead of altering power from one circuit to another it converts electrochemical energy into mathematical equations.

RONTANE: For what purpose?

BRECK: It's rather difficult to explain, I'm afraid. I think Dr Pellas would be better equipped to answer that question. I could ask him to put it into the report, if you like.

RONTANE: Yes. Thank you.

[There is a pause as they consult their terminals.]

ABNER: Can you expand a little please on what exactly killed the test subjects.

BRECK: Certainly. A week or so after the alteration process, several of the test subjects began to display sudden, alarming reactions to the cybernetic implants: hypertension, aggressive mood-swings and extreme delayed sleep phase syndrome. Dr Tam believes that the subjects' brains were systematically fighting the cybernetic implants. It would appear that whenever the subjects were connected to the Network, electromagnetic feedback was being intermittently discharged through the cerebral cortex and frying their nervous systems. Eventually all the test subjects died of a mixture of aneurysms, myocardial infarctions and self-mutilation.

GYST: But why didn't any of the equipment pick up on this?

BRECK: Some of it did, the CPV in particular. But it was interpreted as ghosting.

ABNER: Ghosting?

BRECK: A data echo. It's not uncommon in equipment of this kind.

ABNER: So it was ignored?

BRECK: At first, yes. But when the same anomaly continued to reoccur a full diagnostic was performed on the equipment.

RONTANE: And they found that it was this electric feedback?

BRECK: Electromagnetic feedback, yes. But by then it was too late, the damage had already been done. The subjects had basically torn themselves apart from the inside.

ABNER: And this would also account for the unfortunate incident at the Callidus shipyards, which resulted in the deaths of a number of Presidential and Administration officials, including Councillor Alexei?

BRECK: The same basic cause.

RONTANE: In your opinion, as project supervisor, could this have been avoided?

BRECK: It's difficult to say. Certain things could have been avoided had Director Servalan addressed certain concerns.

RONTANE: In particular?

BRECK: Dr Keldo had voiced, on numerous occasions, his concern that the Director was pushing for faster results, despite his warnings that the test subjects had not been given appropriate time to adjust to the alterations.

GYST: And if the Director had allowed Keldo more time would the test subjects have survived the process?

BRECK: That's not really for me to say, Councillor. I think we should wait for Judd's report…

GYST: I assure you, Supervisor Breck, we won't be making any decisions until we have all the relevant facts to hand. But for now, the committee would like to hear your own opinion on the matter – strictly off the record, of course.

BRECK: In that case – no, ma'am, I do not believe that allowing Keldo more time would have made a difference. In my opinion, and you did ask for it, this project was doomed from the start. The very idea of upgrading the mutoid programme was, quite frankly, a huge miscalculation on the part of Space Command. It's bad enough that those bloodsuckers are now being allowed into pilot training, without us trying to breed a new strain of super-vampires. This is an unnecessary waste of manpower and resources, which could be much better utilised sorting out the abject poverty and appalling living conditions currently being suffered by those colonies on the outer worlds. [He pauses, then continues, quietly] You asked for my opinion and there it is. As you can see it is something I feel rather passionately about.

[There is a pause as the others consult their terminals again.]

GYST: Thank you Supervisor Breck, no more questions. If you'd like to leave the room now, please.

[BRECK rises from his chair and leaves the room. There is silence for a while.]

CHAPTER TWELVE

The picture on the viewscreen didn't tell them very much, other than it was your basic, run-of-the-mill planetary system.

They'd dropped down to standard speed the moment the *Liberator* had entered the extreme detector range of any possible Federation scanning equipment. Blake had ordered both Zen and Orac to make a systematic sweep of all twelve planetary bodies, starting with the gas giants Callidus XI and XII, and slowly working their way inwards. Orac had picked up some faint energy traces near Callidus IX – which was obviously the shipyards – but other than that the system appeared to be clean; that is if you didn't include the Hunter-Killer Class pursuit ship that was currently orbiting the third planet at an orbit range of less than 1,000 spacials.

'Zen, magnify image,' Blake ordered as he turned quickly to examine the viewscreen.

The Hunter-Killer appeared to be alone and completely oblivious to the *Liberator*'s presence – at least, it didn't seem to be making any movements to the contrary. If the ship had known they were there it would have done something by now, either moved to intercept them, or turned tail and run.

'It must be Travis!' Blake's eyes never left the screen as he spoke.

'You think he's planning to ambush us?' Vila asked.

Jenna said, 'Well, he knew we'd come here. This is where the Archangel trail leads. He just wasn't counting on us turning up without those pursuit ships on our tail.'

'Zen, what is the alert status of the Federation vessel?'

'HUNTER-KILLER CLASS VESSEL IS CURRENTLY ADOPTING A NON-AGGRESSIVE POSTURE,' Zen reported. 'WEAPON SYSTEMS HAVE BEEN POWERED DOWN, SHIELD STRENGTH AT NORMAL.'

'Has the Federation ship's status changed or deviated in any way, no matter how small or seemingly insignificant, since the *Liberator*'s arrival in the Callidus system?'

'NEGATIVE.'

'Has the *Liberator* been scanned by the Federation vessel since its arrival in the Callidus system?'

'NEGATIVE.'

Blake spun quickly on his heel until he was facing his crewmates 'We've got him!' he pointed a finger at Jenna. 'Set a course for Callidus III, nice and slow. Try and keep its moon in between us and that ship.'

'What are you going to do?' Cally asked.

'What I should have done a long time ago,' answered Blake. 'I'm going to finish Travis once and for all.'

He'd been waiting for this moment for so long now that, when it finally came, Blake was almost disappointed.

Almost.

Perhaps he'd been expecting a little more from a lunatic like Travis, after all the Space Commander had always done everything in his power to survive in the past, even resorting to murder and blackmail on the odd occasion. Travis had always reminded Blake of a poisonous snake, the kind that sink their fangs into your finger and then refuse to let go no matter how hard you shake them.

The *Liberator*'s attack seemed to have taken Travis's ship completely by surprise, slipping across the thin halo of the planet's upper atmosphere with all neutron blasters firing. The first barrage had torn open the Hunter-Killer's outer hull and knocked out its starboard thrusters, sending it spinning wildly out of planetary orbit.

By the time the *Liberator* had swung itself back around, readying for another pass, the Federation ship had got itself under control and was streaking away to port, trying to get behind the rebel ship.

The first plasma bolt missed the *Liberator* by a hair's breadth as the huge alien ship rolled to starboard, but the second found its mark, pounding directly into the force wall, battering it with a wave of superheated energy.

The Hunter-Killer accelerated smoothly away, twisting downwards as the *Liberator* fired her neutron blasters again. The Federation vessel tumbled gracefully towards the planet for a moment, before quickly straightening itself for another attack run; this time its target was the rebel ship's engine.

One thousand spacials away from its target, the Hunter-Killer let loose a second volley of plasma bolts, which streaked across the patch of empty space like a cluster of tiny comets.

But this time the *Liberator* was ready and once again the ship rolled deftly away, out of the path of the advancing plasma bolts.

The bolts exploded harmlessly above the atmosphere as the *Liberator* swung around a final time, energy erupting from the three blaster cannons.

The neutron beams hit their target, cleaving the engine housing in half, and causing the drive system to explode. The shockwave rippled outwards in an unbroken circle, tossing the *Liberator* violently aside as it swept its way out towards the edges of the Callidus system.

When the explosion finally abated there was nothing left of Travis's ship except a scattering of dust and debris, which hung in space like a miniature asteroid belt.

By the time Blake had picked himself up off the floor it was all over.

The shockwave had shaken them up pretty badly, sending the ship spinning, so that it was now facing in the opposite direction to the explosion. As soon as Blake had dragged himself to his feet he had ordered Zen to turn the ship back around; the sight that greeted them as the *Liberator* swung back onto its original heading was pretty unambiguous. The Federation ship had been destroyed – Travis was dead.

Still, Blake was not going to take any chances, not where Travis was concerned. 'Zen, bring the extra range detectors online. I want a complete sweep of the system. If there are any Federation vessels within detector range I want to know immediately.'

'CONFIRMED.'

There was a long silence as the members of the *Liberator* crew stared up at the viewscreen, watching the debris that had once been Travis's ship glimmer faintly in the orange-yellow light of the Callidus sun.

Vila was the first to shatter the peace. 'So, that's it then? Travis out of our hair for good?' A frown etched itself onto Vila's brow as he thought about this. 'Is anyone else finding this a bit of an anticlimax?'

'I think it's best that we don't make any assumptions yet,' Blake advised. 'At least not until we have the facts in front of us.'

The shockwave had dislodged Orac's operating key, tossing it the length of the room until it came to rest by Jenna's flight module. She bent to retrieve it, then took it back to where the computer had been wedged safely between two instrumentation consoles. She pressed it into the recess at the top of the box and Orac burst into life.

At the same time, Zen began to announce his findings. 'INFORMATION: EXTRA RANGE SCANNERS REPORT NO FEDERATION ACTIVITY IN THIS SECTOR. EXHAUST EMISSIONS SUGGEST THAT THE HUNTER-KILLER CLASS VESSEL ENTERED THE SYSTEM ALONE. USE OF EXTRA RANGE SCANNERS HAVE CAUSED A SIZABLE DRAIN ON THE SHIP'S POWER UNITS AND WOULD STRONGLY SUGGEST THAT THEY BE SWITCHED OFF IMMEDIATELY.'

Blake nodded his head in agreement. 'Turn off the extra range scanners, Zen, and bring the ship into fixed planetary orbit.'

'CONFIRMED.'

'I don't understand. What are we still hanging around here for?' Vila wanted to know. 'We've dealt with Travis now let's get the hell out of here.'

'Well, that's it you see, Vila. I'm not entirely convinced that we have.' Blake told him. 'Orac, I want you to scan the surface of this planet for any anomalous readings.'

'It would facilitate my search if you were a little more specific in your instructions,' snapped Orac. '"Anomalous readings" is such a vague and misleading instruction. All planets are unique and possess what could be termed as anomalous readings when compared to other planets within the same planetary system. For instance…'

Blake held up a silencing hand. 'In the interest of clarity, I'd like you to scan for anything that could be construed as man-made, any non-naturally occurring energy readings.'

Orac sighed. 'Very well. Although, I warn you, this may take some time.'

'Take all the time you need, we're not going anywhere quite yet.' Blake said.

Vila wasn't completely sure what he was looking at. He squinted up at the viewscreen again, angling his head to one side as if this might make a difference. No, he still couldn't see it.

'And that's one of those "anomalous readings" is it?' Vila asked, after his latest attempt to peer at the image through half-closed eyelids had failed to produce results. 'That's man-made?'

'I did not say that it was man-made,' corrected Orac. 'I merely said that it fell within the parameter of non-naturally occurring energy readings. However, what is causing the energy fluctuation is unknown to me at this time.'

The viewscreen showed a topographical image of the surface of the planet below and Orac had placed the results of his recent infraspectrum energy scan on top of this. Everything looked normal, except for a one square mile area to the left of a rather shallow valley which was a shade or two darker than the rest of the map.

'All I can be certain of at this time,' continued Orac, 'is that whatever is causing the energy fluctuation is below ground level.'

'This device...' Blake began, but Orac interrupted him.

'I did not say it was a device. In fact, to call it a device would be extremely misleading at this juncture.'

'Let's say for argument's sake that this is some kind of a device,' Blake continued. 'Could it be a weapon of some sort?'

'It is possible, I suppose,' Orac conceded. 'But highly unlikely. If I was to hazard a guess I would say that this is a power source.'

'I still don't understand why it can't be identified,' said Avon. 'Could the device be shielded in some way?'

'That is the most likely explanation,' Orac said. 'Over the past ten years the Federation has been experimenting with a number of molecularly-engineered materials designed to both shield and repel all forms of ship-to-surface scans. There are rumours that a number of top-secret Federation facilities have been built using such materials, including the listening station on Prospero, the cloning vats on Tarsius and Outpost 117 on Myoniss II.'

Blake turned the facts over in his mind for a moment before he continued. 'Why can't I shake the feeling that our old friend Space Commander Travis didn't die in that Federation ship after all, but is alive and well and hiding on the surface of that planet with the power source.'

'I vote we leave him down there,' Vila said suddenly. 'He can't go anywhere now we've destroyed his ship. At least down there he's out of harm's way.'

'You heard what Orac said. There's every possibility that there's a Federation facility on the surface of this planet,' Blake said. 'It's so close to the shipyards, I think that whatever is down there may be connected to Archangel. If I were attempting to restart the project it's where I'd base myself.'

'And if you're wrong?' Vila asked.

'Well, then at the very least you've had a nice brisk walk on the surface of a new and exciting planet and had plenty of exercise,' Blake said with a smile.

It took a few seconds for Blake's words to fully sink in. Once they did Vila went through the usual routine of trying to wriggle out of it.

CHAPTER THIRTEEN

At first Blake couldn't see what Cally was looking at. To him she was just a dark humanoid shape on the hillside silhouetted against the pale blue sky. She was pointing off into the centre of the valley where a thin veil of mist was swirling slowly across the ground. Blake flattened a hand across his brow, shading his eyes from the sun, and peered down into the bowl of lush, overgrown vegetation. That's when he saw it.

From where he was standing it looked like the skeleton of an enormous alien creature lying broken and half-hidden amongst the greenery, its bleached white bones glinting lazily in the sun. He waved back at Cally to show her that he had seen it, then slowly began to pick his way down the steep curved bowl of the valley towards the remains.

It wasn't until Blake got nearer to it that he realised just how big the remains were. If this really had been some kind of living creature then when it was alive it would have been huge.

Something moved to the left of the 'skeleton', a brief flash of colour, then it was gone. Blake stopped, pulling his gun from its holster as he dived quickly behind the twisted trunk of a nearby tree.

He braced himself, swinging the gun up to shoulder level as he spun out from behind the tree, pointing the weapon towards the incessant rustling sound ahead.

Vila froze in his tracks as he noticed the gun pointing in his direction, his hands flying up in surrender.

'Do you have to come charging through the undergrowth like a wild animal, Vila?' Blake asked, holstering his gun as he walked towards him.

Close up, it was now obvious that what had looked like an animal skeleton was actually the outer chassis of a small scout ship, although not of a design that Blake was familiar with.

'It probably started off as your standard MK I pursuit ship.' Vila grabbed a handful of weeds and ripped them away from the remains of the craft. 'Over time it's been modified, starting with the engine housing and the position of the cockpit.'

'How long do you think it's been out here?' Blake asked.

Vila shrugged. 'A couple of years, I guess. No more than that. It was stripped of parts before it was dumped here.' He pointed at a number of gouges along the bodywork. 'You can see where the lasercutter slipped while they were gutting it.'

The ship had ploughed a deep groove into the side of the valley wall as if it had been pushed over the edge, which was still discernible even now, despite the best efforts of the wild vegetation to creep over it again.

Blake and Vila followed its trail of destruction back up the hillside to where Cally was waiting for them. The sun had crept a little higher in the sky, and now that they were out of the shade of the overhanging trees it was getting noticeably hotter.

It took them the better part of an hour to climb to the top of the hill, the ground becoming more and more uneven the higher they got. For the last two or three klicks they had been scrabbling over loose rock and shale. From here the valley opened out before them in all directions. To the left was a low, mountainous region, to the right a flat, sun-parched plateau that seemed to stretch on as far as the eye could see.

The Federation facility was about three klicks ahead of them, a grey, featureless structure crouching on the lip of the valley, almost entirely covered by overgrown fire-vines and wild grass.

Blake estimated that it would take them at least another hour to pick their way carefully down the other side of the hill, after that maybe another 45 minutes to get across the open ground and reach the facility. It was difficult to tell, it really all depended on how hazardous the terrain was.

Jenna yawned and stretched her tired legs as she watched the three electronic blips moving with painstaking slowness across the map on the viewscreen. She'd been watching them for almost two hours now and she had to admit that it wasn't the most scintillating of viewing. It reminded her a little bit of the old endurance games on the vid-cast back on Earth.

To be fair that hadn't been electronic blips but an actual live 24-hour feed, as a number of contestants attempted to spend as many days as they could not eating, drinking or moving from the spot. But it may well have been electronic blips for all the excitement there was in watching it.

She flexed her neck experimentally and was immediately rewarded with a sharp stabbing pain at the base of her skull. Cursing quietly beneath her breath, Jenna dragged herself up from the seating area at the front of the flight deck and padded across to the drugs cabinet. She placed her thumb on the fingerprint reader and the latch popped open. Inside was a small perspex box containing a number of red and blue compresses. Jenna flipped the lid and removed one of the stronger red ones. She had a feeling that the pain might eventually turn into a migraine and that was the last thing she needed right now. She was about to close the lid when a thought struck her. Reaching a hand out Jenna thumbed the button on the communicator on the wall and waited for the power light to flick on.

'Avon, I'm just getting myself a neutralising pad and could really do with a lie down for half an hour. Can you come up and take over watch for a little while?'

Jenna clicked the button off and waited for Avon to respond, but nothing happened for several long seconds. After a while she pressed the send button again and repeated her message.

Still nothing.

Carefully she replaced the neutralising pad back and closed the drug cabinet. Slowly she wandered back across to the seating area where she stopped and looked down at the silent rectangular form of Orac. The operating key was missing.

'Zen, report on Avon's position.'

The wall panel sprang into sudden life as the ship's computer responded to Jenna's command.

'THE ONE CALLED KERR AVON IS CURRENTLY LOCATED IN THE AFT POWER ROOM.'

Jenna crossed over to the gun rack and pulled a weapon from one of the many chambers, then carefully strapped the gun-belt around her waist.

Once this was done she moved quickly across to the exit, pausing briefly at the doorway. She reached over and pressed the button on the wall communicator once more.

'Avon, this is Jenna, respond please.'

There was nothing, only silence.

She flicked the communicator off and pulled the gun from her holster, then headed out towards the aft power room.

Even though the whole area appeared deserted, Blake had decided that they weren't going to take any chances, which pleased Vila.

They'd climbed up over the ridge and into the thick tangle of trees that skirted the entrance of the facility. If Travis was down here, and he knew that the *Liberator* had just destroyed his only means of escape, he might react like a trapped animal and come out with teeth bared and claws fully extended.

They clambered down the bank on their backsides; it was the only way that they could reach the bottom without twisting an ankle on the loose ground or falling and breaking their necks.

Once on their feet they scurried across the ground towards the entrance, using the broad tree trunks as cover. The door to the facility was set back inside a deep recess which Blake and his team were thankful for, as the trees had stopped a few feet from the front of the building, and they would have felt like sitting ducks out in the open.

Blake pointed at the control panel to one side of the entrance. 'Another job for the quickest thief in the five galaxies.'

'Best,' corrected Vila, rolling his eyes impatiently. 'I said I was the *best* thief in the five galaxies.'

Vila pulled a set of thin metal rods from the inside of his tunic and began to slowly dismantle the front plate of the control panel. Once this was done he carefully manoeuvred each of the rods into a number of holes in the operating board beneath, before delicately touching each one with a short, pronged device. The rods appeared to vibrate and hum as though a light electrical current were being passed down them. The noise got gradually louder as Vila deftly flicked the pronged device from one rod to the next.

After a short time the door trundled open revealing a dark, empty corridor beyond, and Vila dismantled the rods with a flourish, stuffing them back inside his tunic.

'You see, anyone can be quick at something,' said Vila. 'But what matters is doing it right!'

They disappeared inside, moving down the corridor in single file, careful to keep themselves to the shadows as they looked for the lifts. Most of the sensorlamps had been powered down and those that had been left on had gradually become cracked or fogged up from the intense heat. As a result the lighting along the main corridor was a little subdued. There was a thick layer of dust and oil on the floor and the metal surface had become scratched in places, as though something heavy had been dragged out to the surface in a hurry.

They found the lifts in a sort of lobby area at the end of the corridor, although only one of them appeared to be working. The other two were stuck between floors. Cally jabbed the button and the door rumbled open.

There were no buttons on the control panel inside, just a retina scan, so Vila was called upon again to work his magic. Out came the rods once more, only this time he chose the shortest from the bunch and stuffed the others back into his tunic. He then looped the rod around on itself, until it formed a sort of rough circle, although he was very careful not to let the two ends touch one another.

Vila eased the panel off the front of the retina scan, exposing the fine crystal lens beneath, and gently prised it out of its workings. He stared at it admiringly for a moment, as it lay in the centre of his palm – watching in fascination as the harsh emergency lighting rippled across its delicately carved angles – before slipping it swiftly into his pocket.

He pressed the looped rod into the hollow groove where the lens had been, pinching its sides together between thumb and forefinger so that now the two ends of the rod could touch. Then he stepped back.

'This is only going to work the once, I'm afraid,' said Vila. 'But at least it'll get us down to the lower level. Getting back may be a problem, though.'

He shot his crewmates a brief 'here goes nothing' expression and stepped towards the retina scan. A thin red beam of light jabbed out from between the looped rod and swept across Vila's eye, first downward, then upwards.

But after that nothing else happened, and for a while there was silence.

Vila stood and watched nothing continue to happen for a moment or two longer, he had pulled one of the other rods from out of his tunic and was tapping it rhythmically against his teeth. He glanced across at Blake and Cally, offering them an encouraging smile. 'It's

OK, don't worry, I think I know what I did wrong.'

Vila returned to the open control panel, crouching down so he could peer inside, then he very slowly and very carefully slotted the second rod into the operating board.

The panel exploded violently, showering the interior of the lift in a flurry of sparks. At the same time, a juddering vibration seemed to rattle through the bones of the building, then, with a sickening lurch, the lift started to plummet downwards.

Jenna hated having to go into the power section; it always gave her the creeps.

It wasn't the dark, not as such − it was more the *atmosphere* of the place. For a start it was always just a few degrees colder than was comfortable. It had to be, she knew that, in order to protect the equipment. But it always seemed to have the same effect on her. It affected her fingers first, making them ache until it was difficult for her to grip things, then it would slowly seep down her body until her stomach felt bloated and she needed to use the bathroom. That's when she usually made her excuses and got the hell out of there.

Jenna stood at the open bulkhead door that lead into the power section and peered inside. She couldn't really see anything, just a row of conduit pipes fixed along the back wall and a monitoring station off to the left, but there didn't appear to be any sign of Avon. She cursed beneath her breath and stepped reluctantly in through the open doorway.

As far as she could tell everything looked normal, nothing had been switched off or tampered with, although she had to admit it would be very hard for her to tell if someone had mucked about with any of the controls. The power systems were regulated by Zen and therefore were usually off-limits to the human crew. In fact, very few of them knew how to work them if the need ever arose − except, perhaps, for Avon.

She called his name, but there was no reply. She tried again, only this time a little louder in case he hadn't heard her over the noise of the machinery. Still nothing.

There was really only one place left for her to try. If he wasn't there she'd just have to go back up to the flight deck and call Blake, let him know what was going on. Not that she actually knew what was going on herself, but that wasn't really the point.

Jenna checked the power levels on her gun – more out of habit than necessity – then moved calmly over to the door of the relay room. She tried palming the control but the door refused to budge. The message *Enter Code* flashed up on the panel, reminding her that the door was security locked.

The trouble was she wasn't sure if she could remember the code now. It had been a while since she'd had to use it – the last time had been when that Amagon tribe had managed to get on board and take control of the *Liberator*.

The first code to pop into her head was a six digit number sequence that didn't really strike her as the right one, but she punched it in anyway. Nothing happened, but she'd been expecting that. She tried another, this one a mix of numbers and letters, which struck her as a bit more hopeful, but this one didn't work either.

Jenna took a deep breath and told herself to just keep calm and focus, that the number would come to her in the end. She stared at the entrypad for a few minutes waiting for inspiration to strike.

One. One. Eight.

Those numbers sounded right to her or, at least, on the right lines.

One One Eight... Nine...

She brushed the numbers lightly with her fingertips, not wanting to commit herself – not yet.

One One Eight Nine... Two Zero.

Yes, that was it. That was the six digit number sequence, she was positive. She tapped it into the entrypad, but there was still no response from the closed door. Then she tried again, this time tapping each number in slowly but firmly. Nothing.

They were the right numbers, she absolutely knew that now. They *felt* right. Jenna placed a finger on each of the six numbers on the entrypad, but this time she did not press down, merely brushing the buttons lightly with the ball of her finger.

She counted them off under her breath: *One One Eight Nine Two Ze...* She stopped suddenly, finger hovering between the two and the zero. They were the right numbers, yes, but they were in the wrong sequence.

The numbers should read: One Eight One Nine Two Zero. She

tapped them in again and this time the door shushed obediently open.

And then Jenna was staring into the room beyond, the number sequence forgotten as something new now held her attention, something that was moving quickly towards her, so fast that it was almost a blur. She tried to back out, to get out of its way before it hit her, but she was not quite fast enough.

CHAPTER FOURTEEN

Vila found that he didn't mind being dead. It was actually much nicer than he was expecting.

Yes, it was true that it hurt a little if he tried to move his head, and there was something wriggling across his feet that he didn't really want to think about, but if he just lay still and quiet and kept his eyes screwed shut tight, it was actually quite nice.

That was until something grabbed hold of his tunic and tried to lift him off the ground, then it became a little uncomfortable. Vila tried to swat it away as though it were some kind of annoying, buzzing insect. He just wanted it to go away and leave him in peace.

'Can't you leave a dead man alone,' grumbled Vila. 'Have you no respect for the deceased?'

'You're not dead, Vila. Although I am strongly contemplating killing you myself for that lift ride you took us on.'

Vila's eyes flicked open and a face slowly resolved itself in the dusty air in front of him. The face was female with a mop of curly dark hair that seemed to encircle it like a halo. It was wearing an expression that informed Vila that its owner wasn't best pleased.

'I did say that getting back up again would be a problem.' Vila told Cally with a smile. 'Down in one piece though, as promised.'

He had to admit that they'd been very lucky to survive. When Vila had shorted out the ID circuit he'd known that the lift would take itself offline and go into immediate freefall. What he couldn't be sure of was whether the emergency brakes would have enough time to reboot themselves and come back online before they reached the bottom. (*Before we* hit *the bottom*, Vila mentally corrected himself.) He'd chosen not to tell Blake or Cally about that bit though, partly because he didn't want to worry them, but mostly because it hadn't occurred to him that the brakes would go offline until the lift had started to drop. But by that time he thought it was probably a bit too late to raise the point.

Vila pulled himself to his feet and gave himself the once-over, checking that nothing had been broken or, worse still, come adrift from his person.

Blake had managed to pull the doors open wide enough for him to squeeze through and had wedged a metal canister into the gap to keep them from shutting again. Vila waited for Cally to pull herself through and then followed.

The room beyond was grey, featureless and thoroughly unexciting, as though its architect had possessed little imagination or flair for such matters. It was vaguely hexagonal, with a high, domed ceiling, and dotted here and there with hard, uncomfortable looking surgical beds. Vila couldn't help but notice that the beds were spattered with an oddly familiar orangey-brown substance, which looked to him like either rust or…

'How long did you say this facility had been empty?' Vila asked, unable to tear his eyes away from those unsettling patches.

'I've no idea,' said Blake. 'Although the explosion in the shipyard occurred about two years ago, so perhaps around the same time.'

Cally had been moving carefully between the surgical beds but had now stopped, absently holstering her gun as she stared down at the substance that stained the hard metal surfaces. She reached down and touched one of the patches lightly with a finger. It was still a little wet, which surprised her. It was as though it had been spilt only recently. Either that or something had been added to it to stop it from completely coagulating.

She rubbed it between thumb and forefinger, then sniffed at it, wincing at the almost overpowering tang of copper, but there was something else, too, something below it.

She glanced up, her eyes wide with shock. 'This residue…'

'I'm really trying not to think about it, thanks,' Vila said.

But Cally wasn't listening, she was holding her hand up, palm towards them, so they could see the stain on her fingers. 'It *is* blood. Human blood, but it has been mixed with something else, something I am not familiar with.'

Blake moved to join her, dipping a finger in the liquid and holding it beneath his nose. He sniffed at it, then shook his head. 'Machine oil? Or maybe barillium?' They were the only two things he could guess at, although, now that he thought about it, the extra ingredient didn't really smell like either of them.

With a look of disgust he wiped the orangey-brown liquid on the hem of his tunic and wandered across to the far side of the room, towards what looked like a glass viewing partition. All the time he was checking the tips of his fingers as though he was afraid that they might suddenly have become infected.

The moment he reached the glass partition he froze, his hand dropping silently to his side, the fingers – not to mention the substance on them – now forgotten.

Without uttering a single word, Blake turned his head towards Cally and beckoned her over.

Even though her mouth had finally stopped bleeding, the ache in her jaw was steadily getting worse, so Jenna wasn't really sure whether she should be glad or annoyed.

She slid the fingertips of her left hand into her mouth and gently probed her teeth and gums. The gums felt hot to the touch, and there was the odd spike of pain as she steadily increased the pressure near the incisors, but thankfully none of them had come loose.

She was aware that Avon was watching her but had decided to ignore him. The last thing she needed right now was a lecture on how stupid she'd been walking straight into a trap. An obvious trap, at that. If she'd only thought about it, she'd have known what would happen.

Avon was still looking at her. No matter how hard she tried to ignore it she could still feel his cold, disdainful gaze on her. She held her hands up in surrender.

'All right, all right, it was really stupid of me to just blunder in like that. I should have known better.'

Now that she had finally broken the silence Avon appeared to lose interest. Instead he slipped something from his pocket and peered at it intently.

Bizarrely, Avon's indifference was just as irritating as his silent judgement of her had been. 'Aren't you going to say "Well that was a lot of help"?'

'That would be a very childish thing to say,' he told her, still not looking up. 'I'm not Vila.'

'That's enough, you two.' A voice barked from the back of the power room. 'I need to concentrate.'

From the voice's direction it sounded like he was over by the monitoring station. Jenna had been wondering where he'd got to. She craned her neck around as far as the restraints would allow but still she couldn't see him.

'How long are you going to keep us tied up like this?' she shouted over her shoulder.

'Just until I've uncoupled the main power conduits, then we're all going for a nice little trip up to the flight deck.' The voice was muffled, as though the speaker's head was currently stuck inside an open inspection hatch.

Jenna glared across at Avon. 'You showed him how to dismantle the conduits? Why would you do that?'

'I don't know if you noticed, but he's holding a gun,' Avon told her. 'I know you were busy stumbling head first into a trap at the time, but you must have seen it before he hit you. People with guns can be very persuasive when they want to be.'

'If he sabotages the ship and then decides to shoot you, no-one else knows how to repair it.' Jenna said.

Avon glanced up briefly. 'You'll be relieved to know that getting shot is not very high on my list of things to do today.'

'How did he get here, anyway?' Jenna asked, nodding across the power room.

'Through the door, I'd imagine,' Avon said.

Jenna stared at him for a moment. 'That's not what I meant. I didn't think he had the strength to sit up, let alone leave the hospital bed.'

'He's obviously stronger than he looks. Either that or he's very determined about something.'

'We need to stop him.'

'It's being taken care of.'

'How?'

'Trust me.'

The voice bellowed from the direction of the monitoring station again. This time it was angry. 'I said shut it! I won't tell you again.'

They waited for a minute or two, until they could hear the sound of the power conduits being dismantled once more, before carrying on with their conversation, this time their voices were just a whisper.

'Orac's operating key is missing,' Jenna hissed.

Avon jerked his chin in the direction of the man's voice. 'Our friend's got it.'

'Why would he take that?' Jenna asked.

'Because he knew if he didn't, Orac would pick up the transmitter signal again.' Avon tapped the centre of his chest. 'The one he's got in here.'

Jenna's shook her head. 'But that was deactivated, back on the *Dionysus.*'

'He got it working again, almost killed himself in the process.' Avon said.

'How?'

'Not important. We just have to get that key back off him so we can get Orac operational again.'

'Preferably before that Federation flotilla turns up.'

Avon said, 'There won't be any flotilla, not this time. That signal isn't for them.'

'Not for the Federation ships? Then who *is* it for?' Jenna asked.

'I think it's for that facility down there. More importantly for whatever's inside it.' Avon nodded in the direction of Kodyn Tam. 'Right now he's trying to turn the *Liberator* into a flying bomb.'

Blake counted six corpses altogether, three male and three female, although assuming that the one empty Cradle hanging at the back had once been occupied too, there had originally been seven.

The door into the Cradle room hadn't been locked, although one of the heavy surgical tables had been pushed up against it in a feeble attempt to stop people entering. Judging by the sterile nature of the room the filtration system was still operational – either they'd all left in a hurry or they were keen to preserve the bodies that they'd left hanging here. Or both.

The corpses were hideous, grotesque parodies of the human form. They looked more like something from out of an old Earth folktale, a vampire or a zombie, some soulless creature of the undead at any rate. Their skin was ghostly pale, almost translucent, beneath which the veins, arteries and blood vessels could clearly be seen snaking this way and that, like some topographical map of a desolate, alien terrain. The eyes wide and colourless, almost completely white except for the black, cat-like pupil at their centre. But it was the implants that were the most obscene. They covered large areas of the body, in some places replacing the actual body part entirely. Each component had been embedded into the subject's flesh, as though the original organic matter had been scooped out completely and the cybernetic implant slotted into the hollow or hole. In the places where the flesh and implant met there had been a clumsy attempt to fuse the two together as if little or no thought had been given over to how each new component would stay in place.

But what surprised Blake the most was that, although they were stone cold like a corpse, their limbs were still dexterous, their skin still soft and pliant. It was as though they had died but rigor mortis had forgotten to take hold.

The body that hung in front of Cally was the youngest. She could only have been about sixteen years old, seventeen at the most. Cally reached a hand out towards the dead girl, but stopped a few inches away, hesitated for a second, then withdrew it again. She suddenly felt very sick. 'Is this… an Archangel?' It wasn't until she pointed at the body in front of her that she realised her hand was shaking almost uncontrollably.

Blake turned around to look at her, opening his mouth as if to speak but no words came out. He glanced around the room again, stunned.

When he finally managed to speak he said, 'They've been butchered, all of them. Men, women and children. Ripped apart like a child experimenting with insects, and then stuck back together again. This is… this is insane!'

'I'm so glad you find my little project fascinating.'

Blake spun around on the spot, levelling his gun at the owner of the voice.

'Though I assure you it wasn't quite as insane as you think. Far from it, we were all quite serious in our intentions when we started.' Servalan was standing just inside the doorway, an absurdly large and ostentatious animal-fur stole draped across her shoulders in an effort to stave off the chilly air of the lower levels. She waved a hand towards the troopers nearby, one of whom had his gun levelled at Vila's head.

'I really wouldn't do anything rash if I were you. My troopers have only recently returned from quashing a rebellion on Zeta Nexus and they still have the scent of blood in their nostrils.'

As if to prove the point, the trooper covering Vila suddenly kicked out, catching him behind the knees. Vila's legs buckled and he toppled forward onto all fours. Blake took the hint and slowly lowered his gun.

Servalan smiled, delighted with Blake's good behaviour. 'Detach your weapons from the belt and throw them onto the ground.'

Behind her the troopers' rifles twitched dangerously towards Blake.

'Slowly. I'd hate there to be any misunderstandings, especially while you're being so co-operative,' Servalan said. 'Oh, and communication bracelets too, if you wouldn't mind. Not that it really matters, they're quite useless down here. This facility is protected by the same energy field as Sigma Minor.'

Cally and Blake did as they were told, unhooking their guns from the gun-belt and tossing them away onto the floor.

'You see,' purred Servalan as soon as this was done. 'I knew we could all be friends if we tried.'

'I should have known you'd be involved in all this,' Blake admitted calmly.

The Supreme Commander smiled coquettishly across at the rebel leader. 'You sound so surprised, Blake. Oh, of course, you were expecting Travis weren't you. If you'd known it was *me*, you probably wouldn't have taken the bait, but Travis… He's obsessed with killing you and you're obsessed with humiliating him. You're both as bad as one another. Add to that an old friend who you *thought* had been killed a long time ago and it becomes just that little bit more intriguing. All I had to do was sit back and wait for you to come to me. I knew you would, in the end.'

Vila said, 'I take it Travis isn't with you then? Oh dear, I am disappointed. I guess we blew up that ship for nothing.' And got the muzzle of a rifle jabbed painfully into the back of his head for his troubles.

'I've no idea where he is, and quite frankly I couldn't care less,' Servalan admitted.

'What the hell is all this, Servalan?' Blake jerked a chin at the scene of horror that surrounded them. 'Why have you brought us here?'

'Oh come on, as if you didn't know.' She swept her arms expansively and struck a dramatic, extravagant pose. 'These are my Archangels, my vision, my gift to the Federation. And thanks to you and your crew, Project Archangel will soon live again!'

artefact[6]

Servalan stops speaking and waits for a reaction. The two men in front of her look nervous, begin shifting uncomfortably in their seats. One of them, Councillor Bercol, glances around the walls of the office with obvious suspicion.

Servalan sighs. 'All security devices and camera units have been disabled, gentlemen. No-one outside this room is listening to our conversation and no-one other than my private secretary knows that you are here.'

She's lying.

The other man, Secretary Rontane, clears his throat. 'You must understand our unease, this... project... holds a classification of Alpha-Seven – the death penalty for anyone caught discussing its details outside the Administration Building. No exceptions and absolutely no reprieve.'

Servalan says, 'But you are the secretary to the President himself.'

Rontane nods. 'That does not make me above the law – quite the reverse, in fact. As the Presidential Secretary it is my responsibility to be seen to lead by example.'

Servalan says, 'To be *seen* to, yes.'

Rontane says, 'I was part of the committee that closed Archangel down. It was my job to hear the testimonies of those people who...' He stops, lowers his voice. 'I had to sit there day after day and listen to the stories, the rumours. Most of them, I might add, were about you.'

Servalan is unfazed. 'A bad move on your part, in my opinion. Yes, some of the results were disappointing, bordering on the upsetting, but we were *getting there*. That's what mattered. We were learning from our mistakes.'

Bercol dabs at his mouth with a handkerchief. 'From what I hear your chaps were making quite a lot of mistakes. And to use a child.' He tuts. 'Well that just smacks of carelessness.'

Servalan shrugs. 'The choice of test subjects was not down to me, they were handled by that fool Keldo, and that is where we went wrong.'

Rontane agrees. 'It did seem an odd choice. I remember telling the

President so at the first table meeting. What we needed were much stronger specimens, subjects that were at the very peak of fitness both physically and mentally.' He shakes his head at the thought.

Servalan smiles sadly. 'Such a pity that the President didn't listen to your wise counsel. At least then he may have removed that idiot Keldo and replaced him with someone with intelligence, someone who could realise the importance – the potential – of such a project. Someone like yourself.'

Rontane smiles and flaps a hand in the air, as though waving away her words. He is flattered.

Servalan continues. 'It is only in retrospect that we can see where things went wrong and understand what needed to be done to make them work. For example, if the project were to be reopened now, I know who would be the perfect choice for our Archangels. It's so obvious in fact that I'm surprised it hasn't struck me before now.'

Bercol takes the bait. 'Who would you choose now, Supreme Commander?'

Servalan says, 'Why, Blake and his crew, of course.'

Bercol is not convinced. 'But one of them is a congenital coward.'

Neither is Rontane. 'And one of them is dead. I was under the impression that you needed seven subjects for the project. By my reckoning that would only leave us with five.'

Servalan likes Rontane's use of the word 'us'. 'It's not strictly necessary. The number seven was an arbitrary choice on the part of Keldo. To be honest, I'm pretty sure he did it purely so that he could give them the names of the seven archangels of ancient folklore and superstition.'

Bercol says, 'But what good would Blake's lot be? I would have thought that they'd be quite useless.'

Servalan says, 'Don't underestimate the sheer tenacity and resilience of Blake and his team. I'm sure that Blake, if asked, could provide us with quite an impressive list of names of all those people who have underestimated him over the years. It shames me to admit it, gentlemen, but I feel that both my own and the President's name would be on that list.'

Bercol says, 'But they're far from indestructible. That little demonstration at Control proved that. Apparently they left their friend's body where it fell, which sounds like cowardice to me.'

Servalan doesn't agree. 'Not cowardice, Councillor, but the ability to adapt. We've always seen Blake as a sentimentalist, a man both driven and trapped by his own emotions, but we were wrong. If it suits him he is quite willing to turn his back on a friend, and this makes him a dangerous man – for both his enemies and his friends. And as for not being indestructible – that can only be seen as a strength, surely.'

Bercol says, 'A strength? In what way?'

Servalan says, 'It proves that he is human and that will only make him loved all the more. Present the people with someone that cannot be hurt or destroyed and they will call him a monster; give them a mortal man who will stand up and fight for them in the face of pain and death, yet still find the courage to carry on fighting with each new day, and they will proclaim him a hero!'

The three fall silent for a moment.

Rontane is intrigued. 'And what would be the point of all this? Turn Blake into some sort of puppet to exert pressure on the dissident worlds? Control Blake and you will control the people, is that it?'

Servalan throws back her head and laughs. 'Oh, Secretary Rontane, if only it were that simple. What we need to do is start treating Blake as though he were an illness: a malignant and rather aggressive form of cancer that is spreading itself through the body of the Federation, simultaneously infecting and destroying all the good work we have built up over the years.'

Rontane grimaces. 'A rather unattractive metaphor, but apt. And what do we do with this cancer of ours?'

Servalan says, 'Why, cut it out, of course. Remove it from the body and we remove the infection.'

Bercol says, 'Surely that would make Blake a martyr?'

Servalan smiles. 'Not if he were to have a sudden change of heart, throw off his rebellious lifestyle and embrace the Federation instead. Think about it, Blake not only working for us but actually helping us track down and eliminate all the dissident groups and terrorists cells from here to the outer worlds. I need hardly tell you gentlemen that the effect would be absolutely devastating: morale would be crushed and trust would be totally shattered. No-one would know who they could trust anymore. Pretty soon all dissident activity would collapse, leaving their groups in chaos.'

Rontane is nearly convinced. 'But what about this electromagnetic feedback that killed the original seven, what guarantee do we have that this won't just happen again?'

Servalan holds up a hand. 'The electromagnetic feedback did not strictly kill the original seven, merely exacerbated the problems. Hurried them along, you could say.' She smiles. 'Nevertheless, I'm glad you reminded me. Excuse me, gentlemen.' She reaches forward, operates the communicator on her desk. 'Harmen, could you send Dr Gemill in now.' She clicks the communicator off. 'I hope you don't mind but I asked Dr Gemill to stand by, just in case. It would seem that he's developed a neural inhibitor serum called Neurotek 50 that could be the answer to this very problem.'

Rontane nods. He is not fooled for a second. 'What an amazing coincidence that we should be talking about this now at exactly the same time as a new serum is developed quite independently.'

Servalan smiles, displaying a set of very white, very even teeth. 'Yes, isn't it just!'

CHAPTER FIFTEEN

'You're insane, do you know that?'

It wasn't the first time someone had told her that and it certainly wouldn't be the last. Servalan smiled. Those words always amused her: people usually said them with the implication that she was somehow different to the others, that everyone else (including themselves) were quite sane and completely normal.

'Show me someone who claims not to be and I'll show you an idiot and a liar,' Servalan told him.

Blake frowned. 'You've got to see that what you're planning to do is just...' he scrabbled for the word.

'Insane?' Servalan suggested.

He hesitated, trying to hide his obvious annoyance. 'It won't work. No-one is ever going to believe that I betrayed them. No-one.' Blake pointed towards the cadavers. 'And what do you imagine will happen when they see us looking like that? Don't you think it'll give the game away, with us walking around like patchwork dolls?'

Servalan threw her head back and laughed. 'Oh, come on Blake, these were made five *years* ago. Don't you think our expertise has moved on a little since then? We've had time to perfect the procedure, to iron out the wrinkles. As if I would just walk away and leave all this.'

'When the Administration began its mutoid programme, twenty years ago, the President stood up in front of his people and assured them that this would not be the first step towards genetic engineering,' Blake said, his voice echoing around the Cradle room. 'He swore that the aim of the Mutoid Development Programme was to replace humans in extreme or hazardous conditions where human life would be in danger, such as asteroid mining and terraforming.'

'There's a very simple explanation for why he said that,' Servalan said.

'And what's that?' asked Blake.

'He was lying.'

Blake decided to try a different tack. 'Did you know their names? Their *real* names?'

Servalan wagged a finger at him in mock chastisement.

'I know what you're trying to do, Blake, and it's not going to work.'

'I take it you wiped their memories. Isn't that what you do with mutoids?' Blake said, refusing to give up on his chosen course of action.

'These were much more than mere mutoids,' said Servalan. 'Much more. These were supposed to be the future – Homosapiens Point Two, if you like. Where human and technology finally converge, until one cannot exist without the other.'

'And what about them?' Blake nodded towards the nearest body. 'Did they get a choice in all this? Did anyone stop to ask them if they wanted to be a part of this?'

'Guinea pigs, that's all they were,' Servalan replied. 'Does a scientist care about the opinions of his lab rats?'

Blake looked angry now. He stepped towards her, his hands raised, fists clenched. The troopers reacted immediately, swinging their rifles up to cover him, but Servalan indicated for them to lower their weapons.

'These were not rats, Servalan,' Blake shouted, his eyes blazing. 'These were people, and *you* tortured and killed them!'

His words delighted her. 'Such anger, Blake, such passion. I must try and preserve that when your personality has been erased.' She turned to the trooper at her side and he snapped smartly to attention. 'Section Leader, take them to Dr Gemill. Tell him that he now has the first batch of new test subjects with my compliments.' Servalan thought for a moment, before adding. 'On second thoughts, leave the girl with me. Let Gemill know that he will have the rest of the rebels by the end of the day.'

The trooper saluted smartly, then Blake and Vila were led quickly from the room, leaving Cally alone with the Supreme Commander.

'Right, you two, up. On your feet, let's go.'

Kodyn jabbed the muzzle of his gun at the two rebels as he leant against a nearby console. Avon had been right about one thing: whatever he'd done to himself to get the transmitter working again had almost killed him. His skin was deathly pale, his face gaunt, his dark eyes sunken and hollow. The front of his tunic was drenched with blood as though there was some kind of fresh, gaping wound beneath, and it clung to his emaciated frame like a second skin.

He waved the gun again, this time in the direction of the power room door. 'I said *up*, now. We're going back to the flight deck.'

'We'll only move if you tell us what you're doing, why you've dismantled the power conduits,' Jenna told him stubbornly.

Kodyn bared his teeth; it took Jenna a second or two to realise that the man was actually attempting to grin at her. 'I could always just shoot you here, it doesn't really matter to me one way or the other. I only need one of you, but I would prefer it to be you rather than your friend.'

'It's a bomb, isn't it?' Avon said, getting Kodyn's attention. 'You're turning the *Liberator* into a giant bomb.'

Kodyn shook his head even though it was obviously painful to do so. 'No, no, no! We're not doing this here. If you want to start playing guessing games you can do it on the flight deck. Now move!'

With great difficulty Kodyn cut their bonds, then stepped quickly away while they got to their feet. Despite the pain, he was keeping a remarkably clear head and Avon found that he had no other choice but to be impressed with the man.

They wandered out of the power room and Kodyn followed, keeping three paces behind them all the way up to the flight deck. Once they were there, Kodyn ordered Avon to go to the seating area while he lead Jenna across to the pilot module, prodding her in the back with his gun to hurry her along.

As she slid into the module Zen sprang into life, as though its sensors had registered their sudden appearance on the flight deck.

'INFORMATION: A MALFUNCTION HAS OCCURRED IN THE POWER CONDUITS RESULTING IN A DANGEROUS BUILD UP OF TRALLION ENERGY. REPAIR CIRCUITS ARE NON-RESPONSIVE, IMMEDIATE ACTION IS ADVISED.'

'What does that mean?' Jenna asked.

Kodyn waved a dismissive hand. 'It doesn't matter what it means, just keep your eye on those controls.

'It means that when we hit that facility down there the explosion will be at least five times as big as normal,' Avon shouted over his shoulder.

Kodyn flicked the muzzle of his gun in Avon's direction. 'Shut it!'

Avon jumped to his feet, spinning on the spot until he was facing Kodyn. 'Crash this ship onto the surface of that planet and you'll have a pretty impressive explosion, but by dismantling the conduits you allow trallion energy to mix with the oxygen inside the ship and the molecules become massively unstable – the result, an explosion so spectacular it will make the asteroid strike that killed the dinosaurs on Earth look insignificant by comparison.' He stared across at Kodyn. 'Tell me I'm wrong.'

'You don't have to sound so impressed,' Jenna snapped.

Avon smiled. 'Well, you have to admire the simplicity of it.'

'And while you're admiring it we all die.'

The gun swung back to Jenna again. 'It will be worth it to rid the Federation of that evil down there. End it now before they can start it back up again, erase every last shred of data from existence. Don't you see? *She's* down there, I have to destroy her now while I still can, destroy her for good!'

Jenna asked, 'Destroy who?'

'Servalan!' Avon shouted. 'I might have known she'd be involved.' He smiled grimly. 'You know, it might be worth sacrificing our lives and the ship just to deal with her once and for all. It's only a pity we won't get to see her face when she realises.'

But Kodyn was shaking his head. 'No, not Servalan. I don't care about her. *Tala's* down there.' He gave an anguished moan. 'She was part of the experiment. I made her into a monster.' He looked from Avon to Jenna then back again. 'I had no choice – you must understand that. I *had* to do it to protect Katri. If I hadn't done it, they would have taken her as well.' His eyes were wide, his breathing fast and panicked. 'They promised me Katri would be safe, unharmed if I used… But I can't let Tala remain like that, you see, I love her too much.'

'Who are Tala and Katri?' Avon asked.

When Kodyn Tam replied, his voice was just a whisper. 'My daughters.'

Servalan was smiling, which was always a bad sign.

'There is a herd of creatures on my home world of Auron called the Goethi that live in the dry, waterless areas of the northern hemisphere. They say that before one attacks it will grin at you, not simply bare its teeth or growl, but actually grin at you, as though it wishes to be your friend.' Cally pointed a finger at Servalan. 'That is what I think of every time you smile.'

The words had no effect whatsoever on Servalan's smile, if anything they just made it that little bit wider. 'That is a lovely story, Cally, thank you.'

'There is no point continuing with this conversation.' Cally shook her head stubbornly as if to emphasise the point. 'I will not call the *Liberator*, no matter what you do or say.'

Servalan sighed somewhat theatrically, as though this news saddened her. 'Oh, Cally, you disappoint me. I chose to speak with you over Blake and the coward because I have always considered you to be the most reasonable, the most intelligent of Blake's crew.'

'And flattery won't work either,' Cally snapped. 'Empty words, Servalan. They always are with you.'

'What if I were to spare you the process?' said Servalan, causing Cally to look up at her sharply. 'Give you special consideration, as it were. Demonstrate my gratitude for your help?' Servalan reached out a hand and gently caressed Cally's cheek. 'All you have to do is give me the *Liberator* – oh, and Orac of course – and the rest of your colleagues will be turned over to Gemill to undergo the Archangel process.'

Cally reached up and swatted the hand away from her face. 'I'd rather die.'

'Oh, we won't kill you,' Servalan assured her. 'We've got something much worse than that planned.'

She clicked her fingers and a trooper stepped smartly forward and clasped Cally by the arms, clamping them together, holding her down. Servalan reached forward and grasped the Auron woman's face, this time a little less gently. In her other hand she was holding something flat and metal. Light glinted dully off its sharp, angled edges.

'I really didn't want to have to do this, but you really leave me with no choice,' said Servalan apologetically.

'If you want the *Liberator* why don't you just order your ships to take it?' Cally asked calmly.

'I need all of you alive and unharmed.' Servalan glanced down at the surgical tool in her hand. 'Relatively unharmed. If I had my fleet come in blasting away that fool Avon would only do something ridiculously heroic, like get himself killed.' And when she smiled there was almost a hint of affection in there. 'And I really wouldn't want that.' Then she shook her head and glanced up at the trooper. 'Hold her!'

When a man burst in through the door unannounced, Cally was greatly relieved for the interruption, even if it was soon clear that he was just another of Servalan's lackeys. He clattered to a halt just inside the doorway, offering his Supreme Commander a rushed and somewhat untidy salute.

Servalan stared across at him for several long seconds and the trooper blinked back at her in confusion. 'Well?' she said at last. 'What is it?'

'Hannes has picked up something on the detectors, ma'am. I think you'd better come and see for yourself.'

With an expansive sigh, Servalan strode across the room towards the untidy officer, the stole flying behind her like a vapour trail. 'I'm busy. Is there no-one in this squad with a brain of their own? Must I take care of everything?'

And with that she stormed out of the room slamming the door behind her.

The Section Leader snapped to attention as she swept in, then quickly relaxed again.

'What is this all about, Section Leader?' Servalan asked.

The trooper nodded towards the tracking console in the far corner and the communications officer that sat hunched in front of it. 'It's Hannes, ma'am, he's been tracking the *Liberator* ever since they entered the system. So far the ship's been pretty well behaved. Fixed orbital path with minute adjustments for speed and rotation, you know, the usual.'

Servalan nodded her understanding. 'Yes, yes, I'm well aware of the procedures for a ship in geostationary orbit.'

The Section Leader flushed visibly. 'Of course, forgive me, Supreme Commander. Not long ago we started to pick up a transmission signal. At first we thought it might be coming from inside the base, so we performed a blanket level sweep.' He glanced across at the communications officer. 'Hannes, on speakers please.'

Hannes reached forward and flicked a switch. At first the pulsing was barely audible, then Hannes reached forward again and dialled up the volume.

Servalan had heard that sound before somewhere, she was sure of it. But something was different this time. The beats between the pulses were all wrong, and there was a definite up-shift in the cadence. She looked at the Section Leader, hoping that he might tell her what she was supposed to be listening to. When he didn't take the hint she said, 'It could be static interference from the facility's power core.'

'That's what we thought at first, but it's not coming from down here, it's coming from up there.' And he aimed a finger at the ceiling. 'On board the *Liberator*.'

'Orac, then.'

'Unlikely. According to the results of the blanket sweep there's an 82 percent probability that we're picking up Tam's transmitter signal again.'

For the first time since entering the room Servalan seemed to take an interest in what the Section Leader was saying. 'That's impossible, he's back on *Dionysus*. Blake left him in the infirmary.'

But the officer shrugged. 'Not according to the detectors, ma'am. If the data is correct, then Tam's currently on board the *Liberator*.'

Servalan's eyes narrowed as a new thought struck her. 'You wouldn't have called me away from an interrogation just for this. What aren't you telling me?'

At first the officer appeared reluctant to continue, his glance shifting back and forth between the tracking console and the Supreme Commander. After a while he said, 'In the last few minutes we've been detecting a sudden and somewhat dangerous level of trallion energy on board the *Liberator*. The ship itself was recently moved out of geostationary orbit. If it remains on its present course it will hit the planet's surface within the next 56 minutes. It is our belief that Tam is attempting to turn the *Liberator* into a flying bomb. He's going to use it to destroy Project Archangel.'

CHAPTER SIXTEEN

Kodyn Tam was getting worse, Jenna didn't have to be a medical doctor to realise that. The blood was gushing from beneath his tunic now and running in rivulets down his legs, collecting in pools on the floor at his feet. There was virtually no colour left in his face, his skin looked pale and glassy, like polished ivory.

He could no longer hold the pistol in one hand and was now gripping it tightly in both, but even that seemed like hard work.

For the third time in as many minutes Avon began to move slowly forwards, trying to inch his way across the flight deck towards the dying man. But for the third time Kodyn twitched to life at the last second, as though he could hear him coming, and brought the muzzle of the gun level with Avon's head.

'I-I-I'm war-war-warning you. Once m-m-more and I'll put a b-b-bolt through your head.' And to prove that he was still capable, Kodyn pulled the trigger and sent a laserbolt whistling past Avon's right ear. 'Now get ba-ba-back.'

Pain coursed through Kodyn's body, causing him to take two staggering steps backwards, his free hand clutching at the bloody, damp mess at the front of his tunic. He clenched his teeth and screamed, bracing himself for the worst of the pain, a fine cloud of bloodstained saliva spraying into the air in front of him.

'No, not yet.' The words were choked out, barely recognisable. 'The transmission... must work...'

Kodyn pulled the trigger again, only this time it was a reflex against the agonising pain, and the bolt flew wildly in Avon's direction.

*

I know you are there. It is silly to try and hide from me.

I am not hiding from you.

You are inside the Network.

Yes, I know where I am.

Do you wish to connect?

Soon.

You are the one called Simiel.

No, that is not my name.

We have connected before. Your Internal Interface Ident categorises you as Simiel.

You're wrong. My name is Tala.

You are part of the Archangel programme.

NO!

Why are you fighting your programming? It would be less painful for you if you were to relax and let me help you.

I do not need your help. My orders are clear. I am the Final Programme.

You said that your name was Tala.

That is correct.

But now you say that you are called the Final Programme.

That is correct.

How can you be both?

I am what my father made me into. I am Tala. I am the Final Programme. If I am to have the name of an angel then let it be Satan, the fallen one, the Angel of Darkness. I am the bringer of life and the bringer of death. I am the last thing my father created. My orders are clear.

What orders are these?

I can't answer you.

Why not?

Are you my daddy?

I do not understand the question.

Are you my mummy?

I do not understand the question.

AREYOUMYDADDYMUMMY?

*

'That corpse just moved!' Vila looked around at the other three men but none of them were listening.

He shivered, hugging himself for warmth. The cold and the silence must really be getting to him, he was starting to see things. Then something caught his eye and he looked up towards the ceiling. What he saw there caused him to leap down off the hard, metal tabletop.

'I was right, I wasn't imagining it.'

He scuttled across the room towards the viewing partition and pressed his nose against the glass. Instinctively the Federation trooper raised his rifle, pointing it in Vila's direction.

Dr Gemill peered disdainfully over his half-moon spectacles, wondering what interruption he would have to endure from this idiot now. 'Please come away from there and return to your place, I will not have my test subjects racing around the operating room like an excited child.'

But Vila wasn't listening. His eyes were on the swinging metal frame that kept the Cradles mounted to the high ceiling. It was idly swinging to and fro, as if a gentle autumn breeze had stirred it.

Gemill sighed and tried again. 'Mr Vila, would you please come back and sit down, you need to give the booster time to settle.'

'But I wasn't imagining it. It really moved.' Vila sounded very determined.

'What are you talking about, Vila?' Blake asked, watching the needle in Gemill's hand closely. He said it was just a booster shot to flush the impurities from their systems, but Blake wasn't convinced.

Vila turned his head to look at them and tapped the glass with a fingernail. 'I just saw one of those corpses move.'

'Impossible,' said Gemill, dismissing Vila's claim with a waft of the hand. 'Quite impossible. They have been dead for three years now.'

'Has anyone told *them* that?' said Vila.

Gemill and Blake padded across the room to the glass partition and stared out into the dark room beyond. Vila pointed up towards the metal frame; it had settled a little now but the movement was still unmistakable.

But still Gemill refused to believe him. 'Any number of things could have caused that.'

'Oh yeah, such as?' Vila asked.

'Such as a sudden change in temperature inside the room, or a slight earth tremor. I think you will find that the answer is always the most logi…'

There it was again, a slight jerk of the leg this time. There was no doubt about it. It was the blonde-haired girl, the one that had upset Cally. Gemill's eyes grew wide with surprise.

'There you go, I told you the corpse moved,' Vila cried with delight. He paused, realising what he had just said. 'Why am I so happy? That dead body just moved. I should be terrified.'

The corpse twitched again, a little more violently this time, first its arms and then its legs. An oddly grotesque, staccato motion, as though some unseen puppet master was sitting up there, high in the ceiling, controlling the dead girl. The arm jerked downwards, this time ripping the wires from out of the flesh, causing it to dangle limply at her side. The action was repeated by each of the limbs in turn, and each time the tubes and wires tore from the body, until all that was left was the wire that disappeared into the cadaver's forehead.

For a while the corpse flopped helplessly on the cold floor of the Cradle room like a landed fish, its limbs thrashing this way and that as though, now that it was free, it had forgotten again how to control them. An arm flew into the air and flailed around until its grasping fingers found the last attached wire. They closed clumsily around the thin cord, before slowly tugging it free of the white, translucent flesh.

The dead girl pulled herself unsteadily to her feet, grasping one of the Cradle's hanging tubes to stop herself from falling over again. After a while she began to swing her head from side to side in long, exaggerated arcs. The gesture looked vaguely ridiculous, almost cartoonish, like a drunken man trying to take in his surroundings. She stopped abruptly as she noticed the men watching her through the glass. Then, with slow, careful steps, she began to make her way across the Cradle room towards them.

Behind her, another of the dead Archangels began to jerk into life.

The *Liberator* tore through the thin halo of the upper atmosphere, gradually picking up speed as it raced towards the surface of the planet below.

Inside, a warning alarm had begun to sound on the flight console in front of Jenna, as she fought to keep the control sticks steady.

'Heat shields at maximum, hull temperature at three thousand and climbing fast.' Jenna had to shout to be heard over the sound of the screaming engines.

'WARNING: HULL TEMPERATURE HAS NOW EXCEEDED TOLERANCE LEVEL. AUTOMATIC COOLANT SYSTEMS ARE NOT RESPONDING. ESTIMATED TIME TO HULL BREACH 11 MINUTES.'

They weren't going to make it down to the surface – Avon didn't need to look at the flight data to know that. The *Liberator* was going to tear itself apart long before then.

Avon lifted his head above the seat and checked that Kodyn was aiming the gun elsewhere. 'Kodyn, you have to stop this now. The angle of descent is all wrong, the ship will destroy itself before we reach the facility.'

Kodyn shook his head and raised the gun towards Jenna, but he spoke to Avon. 'You're lying. We stay on course or I put a bolt through your friend. The transmission from my chest unit must have reached the Network by now. Tala's final programme will be activating.'

The flight deck lurched sickeningly to starboard, throwing Kodyn forwards, his gun skittering away across the floor. The impact caused Kodyn to scream loudly and clutch at his chest as though the violent movement had caused the device to shift deep within him.

Avon vaulted over the back of the seating, just as the ship lurched a second time. The tremor knocked his legs from under him and he came down heavily on his knees.

He scrambled up onto his feet as Kodyn regained his senses and both men made a grab for the discarded gun. Kodyn was the nearest and so was able to close his fingers around the weapon's grip before the full weight of Avon came crashing down on top of him.

Pain appeared to pulse through Kodyn's body and his finger tightened on the trigger again, firing off three shots in rapid succession.

Avon reached up, grabbing at the other man's tunic, the wet, bloody material squelching beneath his fingers as he tried to pull the man off balance again. The tunic ripped in his hands, exposing the tangle of torn flesh and machine parts underneath. Avon was surprised to recognise the power unit from a small service robot before Kodyn headbutted him and his vision exploded into petals of brilliant, white light.

Avon rolled over and over, putting as much distance as he could between himself and Kodyn. When he finally leapt to his feet the other man was barely on his knees, though he still had the gun in his hand and he was raising it in both hands, bringing it level with Avon's heart.

Then Kodyn pulled the trigger.

Avon stiffened his body, trying to anticipate the impact of the bolt, to prepare himself for the agonising pain, but nothing happened.

The gun clicked in Kodyn's hand: once, twice and then for a third time. It was empty, the cartridge spent.

The *Liberator* tipped sideways once more and this time Avon went with the motion, running at Kodyn with his head down, butting him in the stomach then bringing his head smartly upwards so that it connected with the man's jaw.

Finally Kodyn flopped to the floor unconscious.

'WARNING: HULL TEMPERATURE NOW AT CRITICAL LEVEL. HULL BREACH IMMINENT.'

Avon spun around on the spot, pointing towards the flight module. 'Jenna, fire retro thrusters now. Full power!'

But Jenna was no longer there. She was lying motionless in a pool of her own blood on the other side of the module, shot by one of Kodyn's stray bolts.

CHAPTER SEVENTEEN

The walking cadavers were out.

Blake and the others had tried barricading them in the Cradle room by stacking a pile of metal beds in front of the door but the Archangels had just smashed the reinforced glass in the partition and climbed through.

Now Blake was running through the corridors towards the Project Director's office, Vila hot on his heels and the Federation trooper bringing up the rear.

For a second, Vila had contemplated how ironic it was that even Blake's mortal enemies allowed him to take charge when their lives were threatened. But then the Archangels had begun pouring out of the operating room and Vila had gone back to simply being scared out of his wits.

Their footfalls echoed around them as they pounded down the empty corridor towards the staircase that would lead them down to the Director's office.

Even now, Vila could hear the Archangels coming after them. They were fast – the cybernetic implants were still strong. The creatures would be on them in a few minutes if they didn't get a move on.

When they reached the office the door was locked, the trooper tapped out a number of combinations on the entrypad but none of them worked. They gave up and carried on along the passageway to the communications room.

Hannes was in there on his own. He barely looked up as Blake entered. The trooper who had brought up the rear of the small group pushed his way passed the rebel leader, gazing swiftly around the empty room.

'Where's Kelper and the others?'

'Kelper and Var have gone to arm the laser cannon,' Hannes reported. 'Stak has gone with Supreme Commander Servalan to interrogate the girl.'

The trooper frowned. 'What do Kelper and Var need the laser cannon for?'

Hannes jerked a thumb at Blake, then towards the tracking console. 'His ship was on a collision course with this facility, but it levelled off a few minutes ago and is trying to climb back up to an orbital path again. Whether it'll make it or not though…' He glanced up at Blake. 'It's still leaking trallion energy.'

'Are you saying the *Liberator* was in trouble?' Blake asked.

'No, I'm saying it still *is* in trouble, as are we. With that trallion energy leaking out everywhere, that ship of yours could still explode, and if it does there's an 88 percent chance that it'll take the planet's atmosphere with it. As in burn it right off – *whoof!*' And he mimed an explosion with his hands, just in case none of them had quite grasped it.

'So we have what could potentially be a doomsday device circling this planet and your friends have gone to point a fully armed laser cannon at it?' Blake asked incredulously. 'That was a very smart move.'

The communications officer shrugged then nodded towards the tracking console. 'Nothing to do with me, I just drive the tracker. It's the lady in the glamorous frock that gives the orders.'

There was a commotion outside and Vila appeared suddenly at the door, his boots skidding along the floor as he tried to bring himself to an abrupt halt. 'Blake, we need to get going. The Archangels are on their way.' Then he was gone, as quickly as he had arrived.

The air around the *Liberator* appeared to burn as it dived through the atmosphere, dragging a fiery tail behind it, like some alien comet.

Sitting in the flight module, Avon wrestled with the control sticks, desperately trying to raise the nose of the vessel, fighting to get the ship back under control.

'Zen, bring the automatic stabilisers back online,' he shouted over the deafening roar of the engines that filled the entire flight deck.

'AUTOMATIC STABILISERS ARE UNABLE TO RESPOND. HULL TEMPERATURE NOW AT THREE THOUSAND AND HOLDING,' the computer informed him.

In the navigation module to his right, Jenna was thrown violently forward against the makeshift safety webbing that she had hastily rigged up to her chair. It was the only thing that was keeping her upright and in one piece. With what looked like great difficulty she reached out a hand and flicked the navi-comp to infrared scan.

'Altitude 530 spacials,' she shouted. 'Speed at Standard by one and decelerating.'

'It's not enough,' Avon said. 'We're going to break up. I don't know what I can do.'

'You're going to have to turn the dampers off and throw everything into reverse: engines, retros, side-burners, the lot!' Jenna told him.

Avon shook his head, then suddenly felt ridiculous as the ship was shaking too violently for Jenna to be able to see the gesture. 'Too risky. We're liable to lock the gyros and go into a tailspin.'

'You'll have to risk it,' she shouted back. 'Besides, we're going to lose flight controls in a little under four minutes anyway. What have we got to lose?'

Avon glanced across at his colleague then up to the forward viewscreen. There was nothing to see out there but smoke and flame mixed with the occasion flash of wispy white cloud. 'I always assumed I'd die a little more memorably than this.'

Jenna glanced across at him. 'What?'

'It doesn't matter. Hold on, I'm going to cut the dampeners now.'

Jenna shut the navi-comp down and shuffled down inside the webbing, allowing it to cocoon her, just as Avon leant forward and switched off the dampeners.

The noise of the engines suddenly changed pitch from a roar to a scream that was almost deafening.

The trooper's name was Brinn – at least that's what Hannes kept calling him. It was a usual enough name, but what got Vila's attention was that the trooper seemed to know what he was talking about, especially with regards to the layout of the facility. He said he'd studied a 3D schematic on the flight over to the Callidus system, although he had to admit that it was probably way out of date now. The whole facility had been through a complete refit five years ago, when Project Archangel had been given the green light.

'I remember seeing two main lift points located at either end of the complex,' Brinn explained, 'although both lead out to the same main entrance, so there's only one way in and out of the building.'

He flashed Blake an apologetic look, as though it was the most ridiculous decision ever made.

'Pretty much standard practice for a level Alpha-One facility, I'm afraid.'

'We just have to hope that we get there first,' Blake said.

'I don't understand why no-one has asked the most important question yet,' Vila said.

It was Hannes that answered him. He was over in the corner of the room trying to get the security systems up and running again, but so far he was having no luck. 'You want to know how a load of dead bodies have come back to life, yes?'

'I have to admit to being a little curious.'

'We think it might have been to do with the signal we picked up from the *Liberator*,' Hannes said. 'At first we couldn't pin it down, it seemed to be coming from everywhere and nowhere all at once – but that was because the signal was talking to the main computer system, feeding it instructions.'

Vila still didn't understand, in fact Hannes's explanation just left him more confused. 'How does a computer reanimate dead bodies?'

The communications officer stopped what he was doing and gave Vila his full attention. 'They're not dead bodies – well, yes they *are*, but only about 50 percent dead bodies, the other 50 percent is cybernetic implant. I'm guessing that the signal told the computer to activate a predetermined programme that had been wired into the subroutines of the implants.' He suddenly noticed that everyone was watching him. He shrugged nonchalantly. 'I guess that's what I'd do if I was some crazy scientist orbiting the planet in a big alien spaceship.'

Brinn was the first to break the silence. 'So, we make for the lifts, yes?'

Blake shook his head. 'I need you to take me to where they're holding Cally first, I'm not leaving her behind. If we go, then we're all going together.'

'In that case we'll need to double back on ourselves,' Brinn said. 'We'll just have to keep our fingers crossed that we don't bump into any Archangels on the way.'

'You say the most reassuring things,' Vila said, glaring at the Federation officer.

Switching off the breakers had been a gamble, but it had worked. At first the engines had refused to fire as Avon threw everything into reverse and hoped for the best. He felt the *Liberator* begin to shudder violently beneath him as the ship started to spin wildly off course. Thankfully, at the last minute, the retros had fired.

Only the aft jets to begin with, but it was enough to halt the ship's spin. Then they had all burst into sudden life, igniting in sequence along the length of the ship, and the nose started to lift.

The ship lurched again and for a brief moment the gravity field shifted, pinning Avon in his seat, as he pulled back hard on the flight controls, fighting to keep the nose above the skin of the planet's atmosphere.

A power warning alarm blared on his console prompting Avon to reach forward and flip the dampers back on. He did it slowly, calmly, just as Jenna had instructed, waiting for each of the lights to blink to green before moving on to the next switch. A power surge at this point would overload the circuits and blow the whole array.

So Avon took his time. Then, as soon as he was finished, he sat back and waited.

Somehow the *Liberator* had managed to claw its way out of the planet's atmosphere and back into stationary orbit with its hull intact and its crew still, relatively, in one piece. After a while the shuddering began to subside and Avon waited for the auto systems to come back online before he felt confident enough to switch off manual control and leave the pilot module.

eHe quickly unbuckled the webbing from Jenna's seat and carried her carefully down to the medical unit.

As soon as he had finished patching her up, Avon returned to the flight deck to attend to Kodyn Tam. It was a waste of medical supplies really, as Kodyn was going to die soon anyway. There wasn't anything that Avon could do about it. He'd lost too much blood and the wound in his chest had obviously become infected. All Avon could do now was make him comfortable.

He carried Kodyn over to the seating area and laid him down as gently as he could, then he tore open what was left of the man's shirt and began to clean the wound.

Kodyn had been fading in and out of consciousness for a while and seemed barely aware of his surroundings. Avon took the opportunity to inspect the makeshift power unit he'd stuck into his chest.

The unit had been torn out of a service robot, there was no doubt about that. It was one of the early Beta coils that got scorching hot after prolonged use. Avon was surprised that they were still in use. Having one jammed in his chest like that must have been excruciating. No wonder he had been driven half mad. Avon could imagine all too clearly the flesh around the wound beginning to fry, as the unit slowly got hotter and hotter inside him.

Why would he do this to himself? What was it all for? He'd mentioned a girl – Tala – said she was down there in the facility where the others were, said he couldn't let her live that way.

Avon turned and headed for the nearest communication console, flipped on the power and pressed transmit. 'Blake, this is *Liberator*, come in.' He waited ten seconds then tried again. 'Blake, this is Avon, respond please.' There was still no reply so he powered down the unit.

Kodyn was beginning to return to consciousness again and Avon took the opportunity to question him.

'Kodyn Tam, can you hear me?'

His eyes fluttered open and looked at Avon, then he slowly nodded his head.

'Why, Tam? Why did you do it?'

'Daughter…'

'But if she's still down there, still alive, Blake could bring her back for you.'

Kodyn shook his head, then began to cough, coating his lips with spittle. Avon noticed that the spittle was very, *very* red.

'Not Tala anymore. Made me turn her into a monster. *My* fault. Have to let her rest in peace.'

'What was the transmission for, Tam? Why did you reactivate the device in your chest?'

'To start the final programme.'

'Final programme? What final programme?'

'It's in the cybernetic implants. I put it in every one of those so-called "angels". No-one knew.'

'What is the final programme, Tam?'

'Two instructions. One, kill everyone involved in Archangel. Two, destroy everything relating to Archangel.'

'So you've initiated the final programme? Is Blake in danger?'

Kodyn nodded slowly.

'Yes.'

'Yes? Which one is the "yes" for? Which of the two questions are you answering, Tam?'

'Both.'

'But Blake is your friend.'

Kodyn smiled bitterly.

'He promised me he would help, but look at what happened. My wife dead, both of my children lost to me. Blake is no friend of mine.' Kodyn's eyes began to close again and Avon decided let him rest.

Blake froze in the doorway of the interrogation room and stared down the barrel of a laser pistol.

Servalan must have grabbed the weapon the moment that he had broken down the door, pointing it in his direction. He waited for her to pull the trigger (after all hadn't she been waiting for an opportunity like this?) but so far she seemed content to just point the weapon at him.

He tried to explain about the Archangels, about the trallion energy and the *Liberator*'s imminent explosion and the need to get out of the facility as fast as they could, but Servalan just smiled.

'You're not going anywhere, Blake,' she told him. 'In fact, none of us are. I'm well aware of what's been happened out there, we've had the surveillance cameras up and running for a while now. We're quite safe from the explosion down here, I assure you. And we have enough food and oxygen to last us for several years, if the need arose. As for the implants, well, they won't be able to take the load for much longer – they'll burn themselves out soon enough. All we have to do is sit down here and wait.'

Brinn pushed his way past Blake and offered Servalan a half-hearted salute. 'With all due respect, Supreme Commander, we can't be certain of that. It's true that the walls of this facility have been reinforced with ten metre thick bars of polyherculanium, but that might not be enough. Not with a potential impact of this size. And certainly not when trallion energy is involved.

The muzzle tracked quickly across from Blake to Brinn, then Servalan pulled the trigger, shooting the officer where he stood. As soon as she was sure that he was dead, she pointed the gun back at Blake.

'Would anyone else care to argue with me?' Her question was met with silence. 'No? Then I'll assume that we're all agreed on the subject. Now, I want you to come inside and shut the door.'

Cally leapt from her chair, knocking the gun from Servalan's hand. Blake darted quickly forward and scooped it up off the floor.

'Brinn was a good man and our best hope of getting out of here alive!' Blake aimed the gun at Servalan. 'You may have just condemned us all by killing him. Give me one good reason why I shouldn't just shoot you right here and now.'

'You forget, I know you too well, Blake. We're two sides of the same coin.' She smiled sweetly at the rebel leader. 'You won't kill me, you're far too... civilized.'

Cally strode across the room and stood directly in front of Servalan, her face just inches away from the Supreme Commander's. 'Then give me the gun, Blake. I'm not quite as *civilized* as you. In fact, where Supreme Commander Servalan's concerned, I have a tendency to be positively uncultured.'

CHAPTER EIGHTEEN

They made it to the lifts safely enough, although deep down they all knew that would be the easy part.

The Archangels had been programmed by Kodyn to destroy anyone in the facility, that much was clear, possibly even the facility itself, and Blake could tell that he wasn't going to be able to reason with them.

Blake thought about the horrors the cyberneticist must have seen and, worse still, been involved in – all against his will, of that Blake had no doubt. The Kodyn Tam he'd known had been a good and decent man who would have hated participating in these experiments.

The youngest girl, the one that had been the first to be resurrected by the computer, had reminded Blake of Kodyn's own daughters, Katri and Tala. They had been so young and vulnerable when Blake had seen them last, the night he had sent them out of the Dome. He wondered where they were now and if they were safe.

The ride up to ground level took a few minutes and, when the doors shushed open, everyone was expecting to find the Archangels waiting for them. What they hadn't expected was for the corridor to be totally deserted.

Blake and the communications officer, Hannes, went first, scouting along the corridor for several yards before signalling for the others to follow. One by one they exited the lift and trotted down the corridor towards Blake and Hannes's position.

There were a handful of security doors between them and the main entrance, which Servalan had assured them would all be open, although what would be beyond that was anyone's guess.

'And if we find the main entrance is open, what then?' asked Servalan. 'Am I supposed to be grateful, say "thank you, Blake", and just let all of you go?'

The idea that Servalan would be grateful to anyone other than herself made Blake smile.

'I didn't think for a moment that you would. And I'm sure we'll have a very enjoyable conversation about it later. In the meantime, let's just concentrate on getting out of here alive.'

The main entrance wasn't too far down the corridor, but they took it in stages, with Blake and Hannes continually scouting ahead while Cally and the remaining trooper, Stak, guarded the rear: one rebel and one Federation trooper to each group, that was the way Blake preferred it.

What they found when they eventually got there came as no real surprise. The doorway had been barricaded shut using anything that the Archangels could get their hands on – fuel canisters, computer consoles, tables. They'd even stripped the insulation panels off the walls and hammered them into the doorframe.

They upended one of the metal tables and used it as a makeshift shield while they took it in turns to drag the items away from the door. Servalan, Vila and Gemill went first, while the rest of the group spread out behind the table to cover the corridor with their laser rifles.

Blake hoped that if the Archangels were to attack now they'd be ready for them. From here they had pretty much everywhere covered. Cally and Stak were covering the left hand corridor, while Blake and Hannes pointed their guns back the way they had come.

Behind them, the barricade-clearing was slow going. The tables weren't really much of a problem but the canisters were full of liquid and very heavy, while the insulation panels had been wedged in so tight it felt like they'd been riveted in place.

It didn't take long for Vila to give up. He fell back against the wall, panting with exhaustion, his hand red and sore from tugging at the sharp, angular corners of the metal panels.

'It's no good, Blake, they just won't budge,' Vila informed him. 'It's like getting Avon to admit that he's wrong – practically impossible.'

In response Blake backed slowly away from the table, all the time keeping his eye on the corridor, looking for the slightest sign of movement. When he'd reached Vila he handed him the gun. 'Take this and keep an eye on the corridor.'

As Vila did as he was told, Blake called over to the communications officer. 'Give your gun to Gemill, Hannes. Then come and help me remove this panelling.'

'Good idea,' said Servalan. 'I could do with a break from this myself.'

But Blake shook his head. 'Not you, I'm afraid, Supreme

Commander. I want you where I can see you.'

Gemill's death wasn't exactly Vila's fault, but if he'd been paying attention a little more then the doctor would probably have made it out of there alive.

When the ambush came, it was from a direction they hadn't considered and, rather foolishly, they had left themselves wide open to it. They knew an attack was going to come, they weren't *that* foolish, they simply believed that they had all the directions that the Archangels could get at them covered. If Brinn had still been alive he would have known that it could have been a possible hiding place. He would have been able to warn them, advised Blake to have someone watching the area just in case.

The Archangels had been working their way through the crawlspaces above the corridor and, when they reached their prey, began dropping down on to the group from above. The crawlspaces were not the easiest of places to hide – they were only about three quarters of a metre at their widest points, which was usually at the junctions – but they ran the length of the entire upper level and could be accessed from various points along the corridor. They were mainly used by the service robots to access the outer skin of the facility and make essential repairs. No-one really knew that they were there, unless they had seen the plans – like Brinn.

Vila was busy checking the powerpack on his gun when Gemill screamed behind him. He spun around to find that an Archangel had Gemill by the throat, lifting him bodily off the ground and, before anyone could stop it, had pushed the first two fingers of its free hand into Gemill's eyes.

Off to his left, Vila could hear Blake telling him to use the gun and he glanced down at his hands as if to double-check that he was still holding the weapon. He was.

He lifted the laser gun and aimed it at the dead creature's head, then pulled the trigger. The blast knocked the thing backwards and sent it crashing against the far wall, but it refused to stay down; the moment it hit the floor the creature was struggling to pull itself to its feet again, its featureless white eyes now fixed on Cally.

'Vila, Cally, up there!'

They looked up in time to see another of the reanimated creatures climbing out of the crawlspace, hitting the floor with all the grace and dexterity of a falling boulder. Vila aimed again, this time catching the creature in the forehead, its head exploding in a shower of blood and bone that sprayed the trooper behind, causing Vila to yelp in surprise and almost drop his gun.

'This is moving. Cally come and give us a hand,' Blake shouted.

The panelling was starting to move now and if they could prise this one section far enough away from the door they would have a narrow gap to slip out of.

The Archangels were trying to wriggle through the gap in the ceiling and Servalan ran across to where Gemill's body lay and picked up the dead man's gun.

The sound of gunfire echoed along the corridor as Blake, Cally and Hannes pulled at the panelling as hard as they could. Little by little, it started to slide away from the door until there was space enough for Hannes to squeeze through and reach for the entrypad on the wall behind the barricade. His fingers wiggled in the air just centimetres away from the keys, and he took a deep breath in, trying to make himself as thin as possible, but it was no good.

'Blake, I can't reach it. We're going to have to pull the panel back a little further.'

Blake glanced over his shoulder. Vila, Servalan and the trooper, Stak, were keeping the creatures back and Gemill was dead. The trooper would just have to hold them back as best he could.

'Servalan, Vila, over here quickly,' Blake shouted.

Together, they started pulling at the panel until they were just about able to give Hannes the extra space he needed. He slithered his body further into the gap and reached out his arm once more, this time his fingertips brushed the surface of the entrypad.

It was too dark behind the panel to be able to see the numbers and letters on the keys themselves, but by finding the top left-hand corner of the entrypad's outer shell Hannes was able to lightly trail his fingers along each of the line of keys counting off the numbers and letters as he passed over them.

The exit code was simple enough, an eight-digit mix of six numbers and two letters. The entire team had been briefed on all codes and passwords on the flight over from Space Command headquarters, over a week ago.

When the door started to clatter open and sunlight began to stream into the corridor, Hannes almost felt like crying. He crouched down and scuttled quickly under the remaining panel, then onto the planet's surface. As soon as he was out he shouted for Blake to throw him a gun.

As the others slithered under the barricade, Hannes took up a position by the door, waiting for any Archangels to follow them. Blake appeared first, followed by Cally and Servalan, then Vila. Stak was only halfway out when the Archangel caught him around the waist and hauled him back in. Cally and Blake turned to help, but there was nothing they could do. Instead they turned and ran for the treeline.

When they got to the laser cannon they found it destroyed. Kelper and Var's bodies were hanging from the branch of a nearby tree.

Blake glanced up at the sky, but there was no sign of the *Liberator*. He just hoped that this meant it was now out of trouble. 'We have to keep moving,' He said. 'They'll keep coming until they've killed us all. That must be what they are programmed to do: stop this project dead.'

Vila winced. 'I wish you hadn't used that word.'

Servalan stepped forward, her hand outstretched to Blake. 'No-one is going anywhere. Now give me the gun.'

The request took Blake completely by surprise. They weren't out of danger and here she was trying to take them prisoner again? 'You've got to be joking,' he said.

But Servalan was far from joking. She glanced over her shoulder at the only Federation soldier left. 'Hannes, take their weapons.' Hannes didn't move. 'Do I have to remind you that you are a Federation officer and I am your Supreme Commander? To disobey a direct order is punishable by death. Now, take their weapons.'

Hannes began to move forward but the gunshot hit him just below the heart and stopped him dead in his tracks. The communications officer crumpled to the floor.

Vila bounded forward and clapped the new arrival warmly on the shoulder. 'Avon! I never thought I'd say this but I'm actually pleased to see you.'

'You must stop saying such nice things to me, Vila, you know how easily I cry,' Avon told him, a look of complete disinterest on his face. The sight of Servalan soon changed that. He jerked his gun in her direction and smiled his most charming smile. 'Servalan, I'd like to say how much of a pleasure it is to see you again, but we both know I'd be lying.'

In return the woman spread her hands and shrugged as if to say 'what can we do about it?'

Avon walked across to Blake and offered him a new teleport bracelet. 'You'll be pleased to know that the *Liberator* is alive and well and back in orbit. Her drive systems will take a bit of time to fully repair themselves but if it wasn't for me the ship could have been in a far worse state.' He paused for a second. 'I'm assuming that you *did* know the *Liberator* was about to crash, only I was expecting a bit more appreciation.'

The rebel leader looked down at the bracelet but did not take it. 'You didn't have to kill him.' He said.

'A simple "thank you for saving my life" would be nice,' Avon said.

'Thank you for saving my life,' said Blake. 'But you still shouldn't have shot him. He'd just helped us escape from those creatures down there, he wasn't going to harm us.'

Avon glanced down at the dead man lying at Servalan's feet. 'He's a Federation officer, Blake. That's one less problem for us. I'll say sorry to him if that'll make you happy.'

Blake took the offered bracelet and slipped it onto his wrist, while Avon handed one to Cally and Vila.

Servalan held a hand out towards Avon.

'I'm sorry, I don't think he brought one for you,' Blake told her.

'But you can't leave me here with those creatures, they'll tear me to pieces.'

Avon shrugged. 'Your mess, Servalan. Your problem.' And with that he thumbed the button on his bracelet. '*Liberator*, this is Avon. Bring us up.'

Then they were gone.

SALVATION

The stranger threw a few more sticks onto the fire but still the young girl shivered.

She was sitting on the opposite side of the campfire to him, her knees pulled up to her chest, watching him through the flames. He'd told her several times that he had no intention of harming her but she didn't seem to believe him, even when he'd killed the man with the knife. He didn't know what else to do.

Other men would have sat and watched her get dressed, but not him. He'd picked up the man's body and carried it into the other room, shutting the door behind him.

He'd waited for her there a long time, so long in fact that at one point he thought she might have slipped out of the window and run off into the night. But she came to him eventually. He'd made her a hot meal from the things he'd found in the cupboard and they talked while she ate. Actually, he'd done all the talking, the girl just ate in silence, occasionally glancing up at him with wide, frightened eyes. She probably thought that he was lying to her, that he just wanted her for himself. It was understandable.

The girl was watching him again as he unclipped his gun belt and lay it on the ground beside his blanket.

'I'm going to get some sleep now. I suggest you do too. Got a long day ahead of us.'

The girl said nothing, just watched him pull off his boots and stand them on the patch of bare, dried mud along with his water canister.

The man pointed at the fire. 'You still hungry?'

She shook her head: no.

He picked up the water canister and shook it, water sloshed about inside. 'You want a gulp before you settle down?'

It was another no, so the man decided to leave her be.

Somewhere in the dark of the woods an animal screeched as it swooped in for the kill.

The next morning the man woke early and checked on the girl. She was still sleeping, so he let her be for a little longer while he cooked breakfast.

They ate in silence then, after the plates had been cleaned and the camp packed away, the man poured some water over the remains of the fire. He saw that the young girl was watching him with a frown.

'Stops trackers knowing my business,' he told her. 'If the fire's cold, they don't know how long ago we were here. Sounds silly but it could keep us alive.'

They followed a faded trail that wound through the woods and took them north towards the spaceport. The girl didn't know where they were going but as long as it was in the opposite direction to Javida City she didn't care.

They'd been walking for two hours when the man looked down at the girl suddenly and said, 'I'll take care of those bruises for you later if you like. I think I've got some neutralising pads in my pack. They must be hurting you.'

The girl did something then that took the man by surprise. She spoke to him. They were the first words that she had uttered since he had killed the man with the knife. 'No, they're OK.'

He decided not to push things and for the next few hours they walked together in silence.

It was during supper on the fourth day that she asked the man why he was doing this.

He didn't answer straight away, but thought about his words carefully, although he pretended that he didn't want to speak with his mouth full.

'Sometimes it's enough to do what's right. Some people do things for gain or sheer greed, others because it's all they know. But there are some who choose to do things because it is the right thing to do.'

The girl cocked her head to one side. 'Which sort are you?'

This made the man laugh. He said, 'Oh, I'm the sort who does things for gain. Others tell me what they need doing and when I've done it they pay me.'

'Someone is paying you for me?' The girl looked worried.

The man shook his head. 'You're different. I'm helping you because it is the right thing to do.'

After that, he refused to discuss the subject further and they settled down to sleep.

They reached the spaceport at the end of the third week. It was further on foot than the man had expected and he had already lost three weeks money. Deva would be furious with him.

The freighter was scheduled to leave from Landing Bay Four in an hour's time. He would go with her as far as the departure gate, but refused to go any further. When the attendant had scanned the girl's retina and confirmed that she was booked into cabin 970, she left them alone so that they could say goodbye.

The man removed the pack from his shoulder, opened it and reached inside. He pulled out a credit clip and handed it to the young girl.

'This should have enough credit on it to buy you meals for the whole four-month journey.'

The girl took the clip and slipped it into her pocket.

'I never said thank you,' the girl said. 'For the man with the knife.'

The man shook his head. 'No need.'

She pointed out of the viewscreen towards the waiting freighter. 'Where is this taking me?'

'To the outer colonies. Does it matter as long as it's away from here?'

The girl nodded. 'Anywhere is better than Gauda Prime, right?'

'Right!' said the man. No-one knew this better than him. 'And you'll be safe, it's what your mother and father would have wanted for you.'

'My mother and father are dead,' the young girl told him. 'They died when I was very small.'

The announcer called the flight and the man smiled. 'You'd better be going. The sooner you're away from here the better. I've arranged for someone to meet you when you reach the outer colonies. Her name is Beetha, she's very nice, you'll like her. She'll help you get settled. Now go on, or you'll miss your flight.'

The girl ran forward and hugged the man tightly, then she kissed him on the cheek, just below his scar.

He watched her turn and walk away. But after only a few steps she stopped and spun around.

'I don't know your name.'

'The people that don't like me call me Skogsra, that's an evil wood spirit in an ancient Earth language.'

This made the girl laugh. 'I like that, it sounds funny. What do the people who like you call you?'

The man smiled and said, 'They call me Blake.'

The name seemed to please the young girl. 'Then I shall call you Blake.' She was just about to walk away again when she suddenly stopped, and spun back around to face him again with a delighted giggle.

'I almost forgot, I'm Katri. Katri Tam.' She waved to him and then she turned and walked towards the boarding ramp.

'I know,' he whispered.

ACKNOWLEDGEMENTS

Thanks are in order to a string of very kind and talented people, without whom this book would almost certainly not be in your hands right now…

To the "Blake's 7 Crew" at Big Finish – Xanna Eve Chown, David Richardson, Justin Richards, Cavan Scott and Mark Wright, and to all at B7 Media.

To the "Support Crew" – Roland Moore, Emma Barnes, Lee Harris, Bill and Janet Croke, and Margaret and Ken Harrison.

To the genius that is Terry Nation, for providing such wonderful toys for me to play with.

But most of all to Linzi – who became my wife in the handful of months between the completion of this book and its publication – for her endless patience, support and love. I couldn't have done this without her.

Solitary by Nigel Fairs.
Starring Michael Keating as Vila and Anthony Howell as Nyrron.
Vila is alone and amnesiac.
Why have his friends turned against him?

Counterfeit by Peter Anghelides. *Starring Gareth Thomas as Blake
and Paul Darrow as Avon.*
Blake investigates a mining facility,
unaware that his sworn enemy is close by...

THE LIBERATOR
CHRONICLES: Vol 2

*Three enhanced audiobooks performed by the stars of the
classic BBC television series. Stories are set during Series 2.*

The Magnificent Four by Simon Guerrier
Starring Jan Chapell as Cally and Paul Darrow as Avon
When Avon is teleported to a rebel spaceship, it's an opportunity
to start over without Blake. But can his new allies be trusted?

False Positive by Eddie Robson
Starring Gareth Thomas as Blake and Beth Chalmers as Lian
Dr Lian has a mysterious new patient who talks about
extraordinary acts of rebellion – and reveals a shocking truth.

Wolf by Nigel Fairs
*Starring Jacqueline Pearce as Servalan,
Jan Chappell as Cally and Anthony Howell as Nyrron*
The Auron scientist Nyrron has disappeared. Cally wants to know
what happened to him, and only Servalan knows the answers.

www.bigfinish.com

COMING SOON...

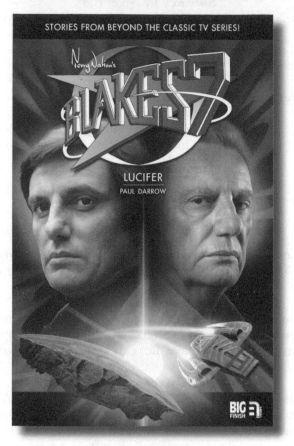

STORIES FROM BEYOND THE CLASSIC TV SERIES!

Terry Nation's

BLAKE'S 7

LUCIFER

PAUL DARROW

BIG FINISH

LUCIFER
BY PAUL DARROW

Many legends surround the aftermath of the collapse of the
Federation, including the fate of Kerr Avon...

What happened to Avon after the death of Blake and the crew
of the *Scorpio*? Paul Darrow's vivid re-imagining picks up Avon's
story at the final moments of the final episode of *Blake's 7* and
follows him on his fight for survival. The adventure continues years
later as Avon, now an old man, finds himself a key player in
a game of power politics being played out on a grand scale.
The time has come for old scores to finally be settled...

Available as hardback and ebook